Star Bright

also by susannah nix

STARSTRUCK SERIES

Star Bright

Fallen Star

Rising Star

Lucky Star

CHEMISTRY LESSONS SERIES

Remedial Rocket Science

Intermediate Thermodynamics

Advanced Physical Chemistry

Applied Electromagnetism

Experimental Marine Biology

Elementary Romantic Calculus

KING FAMILY SERIES

My Cone and Only

Cream and Punishment

Pint of Contention

A Starstruck Romance

Star Bright

USA TODAY BESTSELLING AUTHOR
SUSANNAH NIX

Haver Street Press

STAR BRIGHT. Copyright © 2022 by Susannah Nix

FIRST EDITION: April 2022

ISBN: 978-1-950087-14-3

Haver Street Press | 448 W. 19th St., Suite 407 | Houston, TX 77008

Edited by Julia Ganis, www.juliaedits.com

Cover Design by Cover Ever After

For everyone who's tired of trying to be strong all the time.

one

"HOW ABOUT A ROM-COM?"

Kimberleigh Cress looked up from tying her shoelaces and scowled at her assistant. "No way. Pass."

"Why do you hate rom-coms so much?" Luna shook her head as she shifted aside the stack of scripts she'd been pawing through. There were scripts piled all around her on Kimberleigh's couch and covering the surface of the coffee table, sorted by some mystifying system that only Luna understood. Her eyes glinted with wry humor as they lifted to her boss. "Is it because your heart is a shriveled husk of dark matter that's incapable of either absorbing or emitting light and therefore impossible for most humans to detect?"

In addition to being her assistant, Luna Marquez was one of a very small group of people who Kimberleigh trusted enough to consider a friend. They'd been friends for years before Kimberleigh started making enough money to hire her as her assistant, which meant Luna felt free to shit-talk her to her face.

Some people might consider that a downside of having

a friend in your employ, but Kimberleigh had always considered it a bonus. There were enough people in her life devoted to kissing her ass and fawning over her. She liked having someone around who wasn't afraid to piss her off by telling the truth.

"I don't hate rom-coms," Kimberleigh said, suppressing the urge to smile. "I just don't want to be in one."

"Sure." Luna nodded, tucking a strand of raven hair behind her ear as she reached for another stack of scripts. "Who wouldn't want to be part of the magical formula of romance and comedy joined together in a cinematic perfect storm of happiness? Oh, that's right—" She directed a raised eyebrow at Kimberleigh. "You."

"Name the last rom-com you saw in a theater."

Luna scratched her head, frowning as she thought about it.

"I rest my case," Kimberleigh said.

Luna licked her finger and flipped through the next script on the stack. "I'm telling you, rom-coms are about to make a comeback. I've seen at least two dozen in here, which is more than you've ever gotten before. Everything's a cycle, right? You could lead the new rom-com boom."

"Do you know what the shelf life is for actresses who get pigeonholed into rom-coms?" Kimberleigh shook her head as she adjusted her boobs inside her sports bra. "I'm practically too old already."

Luna rolled her eyes. "Whatevs."

To the rest of the world, Kimberleigh Cress, one of Hollywood's hottest young actresses and star of the smash hit *Otherwhere* franchise, was a mere twenty-two years old. But Luna was privy to all of Kimberleigh's secrets, including her real name, Leah Krasny, and the fact that she was actually twenty-seven.

"I need to take on some roles that aren't about my looks." She'd gotten famous by playing teenagers, but she needed to move into adult roles, and she needed to do it strategically in order to maximize her career longevity. Lying about her age had bought her an extra five years, but those five years would be gone in the blink of an eye.

"This is the movie biz, my dude. There's no such thing."

Kimberleigh stood up and dropped into a hip flexor stretch. "You know what I mean. A part with weight to it where I can stretch myself and do some real acting. I have to remind people there's more to me than a pretty face and a pair of perky tits shoved into a tight costume."

She didn't just want to be the next Emma Stone or Jennifer Lawrence. She wanted to be the next Charlize Theron or Amy Adams—someone who was still landing primo roles well into her forties and hopefully beyond.

At Luna's uncharacteristic silence, Kimberleigh turned her head and caught her friend frowning at her. "What?"

"Are you sure you should be doing this run today?"

"I'm fine."

"You just got back from three weeks of nonstop press tour appearances immediately after wrapping up a brutal four-month shoot in London. You're jet-lagged, peopled out, and I'll bet you haven't slept more than ten hours total over the last three days. You are definitely not fine. I think you should bail."

Kimberleigh shook her head as she switched legs to stretch her other hip. "It's for charity. Bailing is a bad look."

"We'll tell them you strained your Achilles tendon or something. It's no big deal."

"It's a leisurely three-mile jog along the beach, not an Ironman triathlon." Kneeling on the floor, Kimberleigh pushed herself up into downward-facing dog to stretch her calves. "It'll be relaxing."

"Yeah, just you and a few thousand strangers all crushed together and running in a giant pack while a nonzero number of them try to creep on you. Sounds super relaxing."

"It's not that bad. And I'll have Syed with me."

Syed was part of Kimberleigh's security team. She didn't always take bodyguards when she ventured out in public, but given the crowd expected at the run today, her trusted assistant had insisted on it.

Luna chewed on her lip, clearly not mollified. "At least skip the afterparty tonight. You don't need the hassle of doing full hair and makeup after the race so you can stand around in heels and Spanx making small talk all night. Come home and change into pajamas instead. Go to bed early. Get some actual sleep for a change."

Sitting back on her heels, Kimberleigh directed a resolute look at her friend. "People paid a lot of money for tickets to this gala so they could socialize with celebrities. I made a commitment to attend and I plan to honor it."

She'd acquired a reputation for being chilly and unapproachable, which didn't ordinarily bother her. It could be useful, especially as a young, attractive woman, for people to be a little afraid of her. But she couldn't afford to be seen as unprofessional on top of that. That would get her labeled as *difficult*, which was the kiss of death for a woman.

In order to earn her perceived arrogance, Kimberleigh needed to be flawless. Reliable. Unimpeachable. So she didn't flake on her commitments. Ever.

Luna arched an eyebrow. "You realize that ballroom will be crawling with fans trying to get a piece of you?"

"I'll only venture out of the VIP area long enough to give a few hugs and pose for a few selfies before making an early exit." The doorbell rang, and Kimberleigh tossed an eye roll over her shoulder as she went to let Syed in. "Stop worrying about me, Mom. It'll be fine."

NOTHING SAID CHRISTMAS IN LA LIKE A RUN ALONG THE beach with three thousand people wearing Santa hats and battery-operated twinkle lights. It was sunny and sixty degrees in Santa Monica on the late December day chosen for the Tinsel & Tatas 5K, perfect weather for a little exercise in the great outdoors.

Unfortunately, Luna might have been right about Kimberleigh pushing herself too hard lately. She hadn't been sleeping well—but then when did she ever?—and the nonstop travel, interviews, photo calls, and press junkets of the last few weeks had taken a lot out of her. Possibly more than she'd appreciated. It probably didn't help that she'd skipped breakfast this morning as well.

Kimberleigh chose to blame low blood sugar for the unexpected dizziness and nausea she began experiencing in the last half mile of the race.

"You need to walk?" Syed asked, cutting a worried glance her way as her pace began to falter.

Kimberleigh shook her head, waving off his concern. She did not need to walk. She was in excellent physical condition, goddammit. She would not be undone by a short run to the pier and back. Not when she was out in public surrounded by cell phone cameras.

The faster she finished this godforsaken race, the faster she could get out of the public eye. She'd be fine as soon as she got somewhere there weren't so many people looking at her. And maybe ate a protein bar.

To add insult to injury, Spencer fucking Devlin—entertainment reporter, television personality, and all-around slimeball—jogged past her as easily as Usain Bolt doing a hundred-yard dash at an elementary school field day. Looking infuriatingly fit and perky, not a perfect hair out of place or a hint of sweat on his camera-friendly face, he had the nerve to offer her a jaunty wave as he left her in his dust.

Asshole.

The last time Spencer had interviewed Kimberleigh, during the press tour for the first *Otherwhere* movie, his questions had focused exclusively on her body, the diet she'd used to achieve the "perfect shape," and her sixteen-year-old character's form-fitting costume—including the type of undergarments she'd worn with it. His obnoxious interrogation had baited her into sniping back, and clips of their verbal sparring had gone viral, turning an uncomfortable question about her underwear into a trending topic.

After the interview, she'd instructed her publicist to blacklist Spencer Devlin, and hadn't spoken to him since. Kimberleigh nursed her grudges like the children she never planned to have. There was no way she'd let a sleazy dickhead like that show her up, whether it was during an interview or at a charity race.

Digging into her reserves of stubbornness, she put on a burst of speed and forced a smile onto her face for the last eight hundred yards of the course.

As soon as she crossed the finish line, she bent over and propped her hands on her thighs, trying to catch her breath. Syed helpfully positioned his sizable body between her and most of the photographers, though some of them had no doubt managed to snap a few unflattering shots of her that would probably appear in the tabloids alongside breathless speculation about her "secret illness" or some other made-up garbage.

"You okay?" Syed asked.

Kimberleigh straightened, ignoring the resulting head rush and surge of queasiness as she forced another smile. "Just a little dehydrated is all."

"Dehydration's no joke. Do you want me to flag down a paramedic?"

"God no." She could imagine the headlines. *Fragile starlet's dramatic collapse fuels rumors of eating disorder/too much partying/secret addiction/etc.* Take your pick of the favorite malady du jour. "Just point me toward the hydration station."

Kimberleigh felt a little better after she'd had some coconut water and a few bites of a Kashi bar. She even pulled herself together enough to pose for selfies with some of the other runners and race volunteers until the crowd started to get overwhelming. When a pushy middle-aged man draped a sweaty arm around her and leaned in too close for comfort, she gave Syed the silent signal to get her the hell out of there.

The burly bodyguard extricated her from the growing cluster of fans, calling for the car to pick them up as he guided Kimberleigh away. His forbidding glare and no-nonsense manner deterred further fan interactions until she was safely inside the car. Sinking into the back seat with a long exhale, she let her eyes fall closed as Syed shut the door on the crowds outside.

"You don't look so great," he said as the car pulled away.

Kimberleigh opened one eye and made a half-hearted attempt to glare at him. "Flatterer."

Syed's stone-faced expression didn't change. It was useless trying to intimidate these security guys. They weren't scared of anything. Least of all her.

"LAST CHANCE TO CANCEL," LUNA SAID AS SHE WATCHED THE stylist help Kimberleigh into her shoes.

"After all this effort? Not a chance." When the stylist released her ankle, Kimberleigh paced across the suite she'd booked at the Ocean Avenue hotel where the Tinsel & Tatas Gala was being held.

Pausing in front of the full-length mirror, Kimberleigh struck a series of poses before doing a test spin. She'd spent the last three hours being smoothed, curled, contoured, highlighted, and stuffed into a sleeveless Alexander McQueen lace gown. Other than the built-in corset—which made her figure look *amazing*—the champagne-colored gown wasn't even that uncomfortable. She especially liked that it fully covered her chest so she didn't have to worry about accidentally popping a tit.

Luna handed Kimberleigh the metallic leather clutch she'd packed with essentials. "Do you want me to stick around in case you need anything tonight?"

"No need." Kimberleigh gave her friend's arm a squeeze. "Just leave my overnight bag in the suite, and then you can go home and relax. You deserve it."

"Whew." Luna swiped a hand across her forehead. "I'm not gonna lie, I'm relieved to hear that. Your girl could use some quality PJs and Netflix time."

"Enjoy it," Kimberleigh said. "I'll be doing the same thing in just a few hours." She leaned in close to Luna and murmured, "Tell the prep team they did a good job."

"You could tell them yourself, you know."

"And ruin my mean girl mystique? I think not." Kimberleigh never yelled or complained or made unreasonable demands on anyone she worked with, but she preferred not to encourage familiarity—and nothing did that faster than letting people think she was nice. It was much easier to keep everyone at a safe distance when they were intimidated by her.

Stacie, the associate Kimberleigh's publicist had sent to escort her through the red carpet portion of the event, looked up from her phone. "Ready to face the public?"

Kimberleigh breathed as deeply as her corset would allow, put her game face on, and followed Stacie downstairs and into the fray.

———

BY THE TIME SHE'D NAVIGATED THE RED CARPET SET UP IN the lobby of the hotel, Kimberleigh was already feeling drained again. Her head rang from the barrage of strobing camera flashes and the relentless clamor of voices shouting her name, vying for her attention, and bellowing contradictory instructions to look one way or turn the other as she posed for photos.

Stacie deftly shepherded Kimberleigh through the media gauntlet, where she was hammered with inane questions about her outfit, her recent breakup with a rising B-list actor, and the newest *Otherwhere* film opening on Christmas Day. Fortunately, thanks to the press tour, she was able to field them all on autopilot, murmuring the same carefully crafted responses she'd been giving to the exact same questions for the last three weeks.

It was a relief when Stacie disengaged her from the last reporter and guided her around the line of ticket holders and through the VIP entrance to the gala. Thank god this was her last public appearance until the Golden Globes in two weeks.

One end of the ballroom had been partitioned off to allow the celebrity guests a safe space to socialize without having to mix with the general public, who'd paid five hundred dollars a head to get in the door. There were no press or paparazzi allowed inside the gala, other than the official event photographers, so Stacie left Kimberleigh to navigate the remainder of the evening on her own.

Kimberleigh's corset had begun to feel like it was strangling her, and white spots still floated in her vision from the camera flashes—either that or she was developing hypoxia from the compression of her rib cage. Hoping a drink would relax her enough to get through the next couple of hours, she headed for the bar.

Annoyingly, the very first person she encountered was Spencer freaking Devlin. While she was waiting for the bartender to open a bottle of prosecco, Spencer sidled up beside her and unleashed the pretty-boy smile and soft Southern drawl he used to disarm the subjects of his television interviews. "Kimberleigh Cress, as I live and breathe. Fancy meeting you here."

She didn't bother to hide her irritation, both at his cheesy affectation of charm and at the fact of his existence in general. "I thought your kind were being stopped at the door."

"Reporters, you mean?"

"Reptiles."

Spencer smirked, unruffled by the insult. "You can put your claws away. I'm off the clock tonight."

The bartender set Kimberleigh's glass of prosecco in front of her. Snatching it up, she marched away from the bar, determined to put as much distance as possible between herself and Spencer Devlin.

Unfortunately, like so many in his line of work, he was as relentless as a mosquito and impervious to social cues. He closed the distance between them in two strides of his long legs and stepped in front of her, forcing a halt to her retreat. "I have to say, I'm surprised to see you here."

Kimberleigh leveled an impatient glare at him. "Why is that?"

"I wouldn't have taken you for the charitable type."

"I could say the same about you."

"As a matter of fact, I'm heavily involved with several charities. I try to lend my support to good causes whenever I can make the time."

She rolled her eyes as she sipped her prosecco. "Good for you."

"I have a question."

Her gaze narrowed. "I thought you were off the clock."

"This is off the record. Merely for my own edification."

"Big word."

His cheek dimpled in an annoyingly attractive smirk. "It was featured last week on my Big Word of the Day calendar."

She ignored his attempt at humor. "Any questions you have for me can be posed through my publicist, who will gladly relay that I have nothing to say to you today or ever."

"You really don't like me, do you?"

"Does that surprise you?"

He shrugged. "Most people like me. I'm a likable guy."

Kimberleigh's lip curled. "I find that difficult to believe."

"Maybe you should give me another chance."

"Why? So you can ask me about my underwear on national television again?"

He frowned, and if she didn't know better, she might almost think there was a hint of contrition in it. "Is that what this is about?"

"Among other things." There was also the matter of his interview with actress Poppy Carpenter last year. Spencer had ambushed her on-air with a series of invasive questions about her abusive father that hadn't been cleared in the pre-interview and ended up making her cry. Kimberleigh had worked with Poppy early in her career and felt a certain amount of loyalty to her, especially given her troubled past. She didn't deserve to have her private struggles made public without her consent.

Spencer's eyes narrowed slightly. "How many reporters asked you similar questions about your costume on that press tour?"

"Too many," Kimberleigh was forced to concede. It had come up a few times on this recent press tour as well, but her publicity team had gotten better about shutting down that line of questioning. "But you're the only one who did it live on a national network morning show."

Spencer nodded. "Would it help if I offered an apology?"

The offer took Kimberleigh by surprise, but she had no interest in an apology. She didn't give a crap about Spencer's feelings or his opinion of her. She simply wanted him and every other reporter to stop talking about actresses as if they were thoroughbred horses rather than human beings. She'd wanted to punish him so he'd learn a lesson and do better with the next young actress who wound up in his interview chair. But she'd also enjoyed punishing him because he was a shallow jackass who'd embarrassed her and humiliated someone she liked.

She gazed at him coolly, refusing to let any emotion into her expression. "Like I said, any questions you have for me can be posed through my publicist."

Spencer opened his mouth, but before he could say anything they were interrupted by Robbie Scarborough.

"Kimberleigh! You look stunning as usual." The handsome actor and former teen heartthrob leaned in to kiss her cheek. When he turned to address Spencer, the smile left Robbie's eyes. "I'm not interrupting, am I?"

"No," Kimberleigh answered. "Spencer was just leaving."

Spencer met Robbie's taut smile with one of his own. "Apparently I was just leaving." His gaze dropped to Kimberleigh, and his expression softened. "Kimberleigh. Always a pleasure talking to you."

"I hate that fucking guy," Robbie muttered as soon as Spencer was out of earshot.

Robbie happened to be Poppy Carpenter's ex-fiancé, so he had good reason to dislike Spencer Devlin. Poppy and Robbie had been Hollywood's favorite couple four years ago when Kimberleigh had landed her second feature-film role playing Poppy's younger sister. Not long after that movie had wrapped, Robbie and Poppy went through a public breakup that got messy after a gossip site claimed Poppy had cheated on Robbie with his best friend.

The gossip site that had started the rumor? Hot Hollywood Nights—the same one Spencer Devlin had been writing for at the time, back before he'd landed his first on-camera job with the *Hot Hollywood Nights* television show.

"So say we all," Kimberleigh murmured as she watched Spencer disappear into the crowd.

Robbie turned back to her, flashing the boyish grin that had launched a million millennial preteen crushes. "I saw him corner you and thought you might need a rescue."

"I appreciate that." Kimberleigh offered Robbie a sincere smile. The two of them went back a ways, and he'd been nice to her before she was anyone important. "I could have taken out the trash myself, but it's nice to have an assist."

"How've you been?" Robbie asked. "I haven't seen you in forever."

"Working nonstop. You know how it is. Trying to capitalize on the momentum while it lasts."

Robbie nodded. "Nice work if you can get it."

His career hadn't exactly been going gangbusters lately. He'd made some bad calls and starred in a couple of back-to-back flops. It had been a while since he'd headlined a box office hit, which meant he probably wasn't getting offered the big projects anymore.

When Kimberleigh looked at Robbie, she saw what her future could be in ten years if she didn't do everything exactly right. It was daunting to realize how easily you could go from superstar to afterthought. That was the reason she drove herself so hard. She didn't want to be another forgotten has-been.

They chatted for a few minutes before Robbie excused himself to go say hi to someone else. As they'd talked, the ballroom had filled up, and Kimberleigh felt the curious eyes of the general admission attendees on her and the others in the roped-off VIP area. It was like being an animal on display at the zoo—stared at and photographed, but protected from the gawkers by the bars of the cage they inhabited.

Still, she'd come here for a reason, and it wasn't to hang out with other celebrities. The prosecco she'd drunk while chatting with Robbie had helped take the edge off her frayed nerves. She considered another glass, then thought better of it. It was wiser to keep her wits sharp if she was going to be mingling with the public.

She recognized quite a few celebrity guests chatting it up with the ticket holders on the other side of the ropes. The attendees seemed to be on their best behavior so far, and there were plenty of watchful security personnel stationed around the room, ready to intervene if anyone got too brazen. Best to get this over with now, before too much alcohol had been consumed and people began to forget their manners.

Depositing her empty glass on a table, Kimberleigh put on her most becoming smile and ventured out of the VIP area. She spent the next hour working the room. Moving from group to group and introducing herself as if she didn't expect to be recognized. Shaking hands with breathless strangers, answering their questions about her movies, and posing for dozens of selfies.

This part of fame didn't come easily for her. She'd always found the parasocial relationship between celebrities and fans difficult to navigate. It was unnerving talking to total strangers who felt like they knew her because they'd seen her face on-screen and read a lot of half-truths about her on the internet.

Unlike a lot of actors, Kimberleigh wasn't a natural people person. She wasn't an extrovert and she didn't thrive on attention. It took a lot of effort to be "on" for people. To smooth all her rough edges and be the perfect embodiment of the person they wanted her to be. The ideal fantasy they'd created in their heads instead of the messy, flawed human she actually was. It felt like walking on a tightrope above the circus floor. The better she got at it, the higher they moved the rope—and the farther she had to fall if she made a wrong step.

As more people poured into the ballroom, the din grew louder and more oppressive. Kimberleigh's smile began to feel more wooden, and it became even more of a struggle to retrieve the appropriate social niceties and keep the small talk flowing smoothly with tongue-tied fans.

"Enjoy the rest of the night," she said to a pair of wide-eyed teenage girls after posing for what must have been her hundredth selfie of the evening. "It was lovely to meet you."

This damned corset had been a mistake. Her chest felt tight, like she couldn't get enough air, and her heart was racing so fast it was difficult to think straight.

Deciding she'd done enough for the cause, Kimberleigh made her way back inside the VIP section. Instead of another prosecco, she asked for a glass of ice water. Her face felt hot and itchy even though it was freezing in the ballroom. She pressed the cold glass to the inside of her wrist, wondering if she was having a reaction to the makeup they'd put on her.

"Look who it is! Little Kimmie!"

Hiding a wince, Kimberleigh turned around to face the former professional wrestler who'd greeted her. "Hello, Chuck."

Chuck Hammer grinned as his massive arms enveloped her in a suffocating hug. Kimberleigh tolerated the middle-aged action star's embrace, then stepped back as soon as he let her go. She'd done her very first film with him, playing his fourteen-year-old stepdaughter. Chuck was a friendly teddy bear, but he still treated her like a child, which Kimberleigh found less endearing with every passing year. She wasn't in the mood for his boisterous personality or chummy teasing tonight. Not when she was this exhausted and barely holding it together.

"Do you know Griffin Beach?" Chuck asked. "He's on

the organizing committee for this shindig and guilted me into coming."

Kimberleigh hadn't even noticed the younger man standing beside Chuck. He looked vaguely familiar, but his generic good looks were virtually indistinguishable from half the actors in Hollywood. "I don't think so."

She was starting to feel sweaty and nauseous, just like she had during the race earlier today. Except she couldn't blame her current state on physical exertion or dehydration. She'd even choked down the protein bar Luna had forced on her in the hotel room while she was getting her hair styled, so it wasn't low blood sugar either.

"You and I are actually doing a movie together next year," Griffin said.

Kimberleigh tried to force a smile. "Is that right?"

"*Prepare for War*? The Jerry Duncan project. We're shooting in Atlanta over the summer."

"Right, of course." It felt like there was an iron band tightening around her chest. Cutting off her oxygen. Making her head spin and her ears ring.

Shit. This was bad. She needed to get out of here. Now. She couldn't let herself be seen like this.

"Excuse me," she said, walking away from Chuck and Griffin as they exchanged a puzzled glance at her rudeness.

She tried to control her breathing as she headed for the nearest door. Her vision started to tunnel as she pushed through it into a smaller adjoining room. It was empty, thank god, and quiet. Much quieter than the ballroom. With no nosy eyes to see her fall apart.

Opening her clutch with shaking hands, she pawed through the contents in a desperate hope her pills would be in there. But they weren't. She'd told Luna not to bother packing them anymore because she hadn't had an attack in months. She'd thought she was past it.

Fuck.

Sagging back against the wall, she slid to the floor and pulled her knees to her chest.

I'm fine. It'll be okay.

I'm fine. It'll be okay.

I'm fine. It'll be okay.

She repeated the phrase over and over, clinging to it like a drowning person clings to a life preserver.

two

SPENCER HAD COME a long way from making pennies a word as a freelance entertainment writer. These days he was a celebrity in his own right: the host of three different television shows in addition to his regular featured segment on a network morning show and his own satellite radio show.

But what he'd learned tonight could be the ticket to unlocking the next level of his career and make him even more of a household name. He'd gotten a tip that a certain late-night talk show host wasn't planning to renew his contract next year. If Spencer played his cards right, he might have a shot at replacing him.

His own talk show.

That was the dream, right? Granted, it was the late-late slot, but still. This could be huge for him. He needed to call his agent and get her working on a strategy. When the network found out their star was jumping and started the search for a replacement, Spencer wanted to be sure his name was already first in their minds. That meant laying the groundwork now, before they even knew they had a need to fill.

He glanced around the ballroom, looking for somewhere quieter and more private to make a phone call.

There. Directly across from the VIP entrance was a closed door. He headed that way and gave it a tentative push. It was unlocked. And the room beyond was empty. Perfect.

Slipping inside, Spencer pulled out his phone and thumbed to his agent's number. Just as he was about to connect the call, a noise behind him made him spin around.

He did a double take when he realized the woman sitting on the floor against the wall was Kimberleigh Cress. As if that wasn't weird enough, the odd noise he'd heard was her breathing—or trying to breathe. Her chest hitched with every shallow, gasping inhale, her whole body shuddering with the effort as she hugged her knees.

Oh, hell.

Squeezing his phone in case he needed to dial 911, Spencer went over and crouched on the floor in front of her. "Kimberleigh?"

Her head jerked up, her eyes wide with panic. But there was a familiar glint of anger in her emerald gaze, which he found reassuring. If she was herself enough to be resentful of his presence, she couldn't be all that bad off. Could she?

"Do you need medical assistance? Should I call for help?"

She responded by seizing his arm in a claw-like grip and shaking her head forcefully. "Don't," she ground out, her voice little more than a wheeze.

Okay, then. No calling 911.

"Do you know what's wrong with you?" he asked.

This time she nodded.

"Is it an asthma attack?"

She shook her head.

He studied her more closely. Her pale, sweaty skin, rapid breathing, and white-knuckled grip on his arm struck a familiar chord. "Is it a panic attack?" he guessed, recognizing the signs of a fight-or-flight response.

Her gaze flicked his way, and she glared at him for a moment before finally confirming his suspicions with a reluctant nod.

Spencer relaxed a little. He knew what to do for a panic attack, unlike asthma or some other life-threatening medical crisis. "Do you have medication to take?"

Kimberleigh shook her head as she struggled to speak. "Didn't...bring it."

"That's okay. You're going to be fine." He spoke in his calmest, gentlest voice. "Is there anyone I can get for you? Or call?" When she shook her head again, he tucked his phone into his jacket pocket and hunkered down on the floor, getting more comfortable. "In that case I'm going to stay right here with you, all right?"

Her green eyes continued to shoot daggers at him, but she kept her possessive hold on his arm. Since he'd half expected her to tell him to fuck off into the sun, he took it as confirmation she wanted him to stay.

"Do you have a grounding technique or anchoring phrase you like to use?"

Another scowl. Another head shake.

Okay, he'd have to improvise. Fortunately, Spencer was

no stranger to panic attacks. He'd had his fair share back in high school, before he'd learned better strategies for coping with his anxiety than smoking weed and skipping class.

"Here." Gently uncurling her fingers from his arm, he held Kimberleigh's palm to his chest above his heart. "Can you feel my heart beating? Try to focus on that."

She glared at him, but didn't pull out of his grasp. Squeezing her fingers slightly, he breathed in slowly and then out again, letting his chest rise and fall with each modulated breath.

"Try to match your breathing to mine if you can. Nice and slow. Breathe in. Hold it. Breathe out again. That's good. You're doing great. Everything's going to be okay." Spencer reached into his pants pocket and retrieved his grandfather's signet ring, the one he carried around with him to fend off attacks just like this one. He gave it a brief squeeze, running his fingertips over the familiar, reassuring surfaces before he pushed it into Kimberleigh's free hand. "Hold on to this."

Her eyes lifted to his, not with anger this time, but confusion.

He smiled. "Just hold it in your hand. Feel the weight of it. The different textures. And keep breathing with me. Nice and slow. Steady breaths. You're doing great. You've got this."

They sat there like that for several minutes, quietly inhaling and exhaling together. Creating a small bubble of calm around them while the muffled sounds of the gala carried on next door. As he held Kimberleigh's hand against his heart and watched her fight to modulate her breathing,

Spencer felt an unexpected kinship with her—and a newfound respect.

Before tonight, he would have described her as spoiled and prone to temper tantrums. Beyond that he hadn't given her much thought. She was just another celebrity, no more or less interesting to him than any of the hundreds of others he interacted with for his job. Someone to be leveraged, who needed him just as much as he needed them.

Except Kimberleigh *hadn't* needed him. She'd shown an unusual degree of backbone, both during that disastrous interview last year and in her stubborn blacklisting of him ever since. She was someone who knew how to hold a grudge, that was for sure.

No doubt she'd go back to hating him as soon as she was feeling like herself again. But in the meantime he was enjoying the temporary truce. Serenity settled over him like a soft, cozy blanket as his meditative breathing and the feel of Kimberleigh's small hand warming under his eased away tension he hadn't even realized he'd been carrying.

Eventually, when her breathing grew less labored and some of the strain had left her face, Spencer broke the peaceful silence. "Feeling better?"

Kimberleigh gave him a small nod. "A little."

He lowered her hand from his chest and rested his arm on his knee, loosening his grasp in case she wanted to pull her hand away. To his surprise, she left her hand in his, her fingers lightly resting in his palm. So maybe not entirely back to herself yet.

He tried lightening the mood with some gentle teasing. "I'm sure you must be absolutely thrilled to have me here, right? No one better to have at your side during an anxiety attack than me, your favorite person in the whole world."

She gave him an eye roll that he took as a sign she was indeed feeling better.

He could guess how much she probably hated being this vulnerable in front of anyone—much less someone like him—so he tried to put her at ease. "I'm not going to tell anyone about this, if you're worried about that. I know you don't think very much of me, but I do actually have some scruples in my cold-blooded reptilian heart."

She cast a glance at him, her expression conveying skepticism. Spencer tried not to take it personally. Kimberleigh had good reason to doubt his sincerity. People like her learned early in their careers not to trust people like him.

But she was still holding his hand. That had to mean something.

Her eyes searched his. "How did you know exactly what to do?"

He offered her a level gaze. "I think you can probably guess."

"Does that mean you…"

"Have panic attacks sometimes? Yes, as a matter of fact, I do. So I won't tell your secret if you don't tell mine. Deal?"

"Deal." Her mouth twitched in the barest hint of a smile, and even that minuscule gesture of acceptance was enough to cause a flicker of…something in his chest. "Thank you," she added softly as her gaze skated away from his.

The flicker in his chest grew into a whole-ass flare of warmth, right next to his heart where her hand had been touching him only moments ago.

Spencer cleared his throat, feeling uncharacteristically off-balance. "Are you ready to get out of here?"

"Not yet." Kimberleigh cast a nervous glance at the door and shuddered. "I don't want to go back out there." Her hand shook a little in his, and he twined their fingers together, squeezing lightly.

"Okay. We can stay right here until you're ready."

She let out a long breath as her shoulders relaxed again. "You don't have to stay with me."

"I know, but I'd feel better if you let me stay until I know you're back to yourself again."

"Thank you," she said again.

Kimberleigh Cress didn't strike him as someone who said thank you very often, so it seemed like a big deal that he'd gotten two out of her in as many minutes. But then again he didn't actually know her well. Maybe the ice queen reputation that followed her around wasn't fair.

"You're welcome," he replied, leaving it at that.

"Why did you come in here, anyway?" She was still holding his grandfather's ring, turning it over in her left hand, running her fingertips over it like he'd told her to.

"I was looking for somewhere quiet to make a phone call."

"Was it an important call? If you need to—"

"It wasn't important. It can wait." Five minutes ago it had seemed like the biggest thing that had ever happened to him, but now? He couldn't imagine leaving Kimberleigh for something so utterly insignificant.

"Okay." She lowered her legs, slipping her hand out of his finally to smooth down her skirt.

Spencer mourned the loss of her touch more than he

had any right to. Far more than was wise, given her enmity for him. He studied her, more conscious than ever of how tiny she was. Five foot nothing and maybe a hundred pounds soaking wet. Not that there was anything unusual about that in her business. She was average-sized for an actress.

But she seemed much smaller sitting on the floor next to him, her complexion wan even through her makeup and her movements visibly shaky. He wasn't used to thinking of her as fragile. She usually gave off such strong "Go fuck yourself" energy that she'd always appeared larger and stronger than she was.

"Can I ask you something?" he said and instantly felt Kimberleigh stiffen, every muscle in her body tensing like she was expecting an attack. "Off the record," he added, raising his hand in a scout's salute. "I swear."

"What?" she asked, still wary.

"Has this ever happened to you before?"

"A couple of times, yeah." She grimaced, her eyes dropping to the floor. "But not for a while. I thought I had it under control. That's why I don't carry my prescription with me anymore."

"Do you know what set you off tonight?"

"Not really." She frowned, looking down at his ring. Cradling it in both hands as she rubbed her fingers over it. "I think it was probably a lot of things building up and tonight was just the last straw. I've been going nonstop on this press tour, and between the jet lag, insomnia, and having to be on all day long for weeks on end, I guess it's taken more out of me than I realized. The truth is, I'm not really cut out for all this peopling."

"You don't say," Spencer murmured. Kimberleigh's eyes cut over to his, and he offered a shrug.

She surprised him by smiling. "I guess I don't hide it very well, do I?"

"Were you trying to hide it?" he asked, only half teasing.

Her smile grew a little, and she shook her head. "Not really, no."

"So it's not just me who's experienced the Kimberleigh Cress cold shoulder? And here I thought I was special."

Most of the warmth fled her expression. "Oh don't worry, you're definitely special."

"You're really never going to forgive me for that interview, are you?"

Kimberleigh's green eyes glinted with ice as they turned toward him. "Should I?"

"Was it really that bad?"

She regarded him for a moment. "You're what—in your mid-thirties?"

He shot her an offended look as he rubbed a self-conscious hand over the back of his neck. "I'm twenty-nine, thanks very much."

"Yeah, well, I filmed all three *Otherwhere* movies back-to-back when I was eighteen. Don't you think it's pretty gross for a man to be commenting on a teenage girl's body at your age?"

"It would definitely be gross, if it weren't bullshit. I know for a fact you're older than you claim."

"Says who?" Kimberleigh had a pretty good poker face, he had to give her that. But he'd made a study of reading microexpressions, and he could still tell he'd landed a direct hit.

"Says me. You don't remember the first time we met, do you?" He'd always suspected as much. There was no reason for her to remember him or the random audition that had briefly put them in the same room together before either of their faces were recognizable. Back when Spencer had still thought he might have a career as an actor.

"You mean last year?"

"No, six years ago. You and I read for a commercial together."

She blinked her improbably long lashes in surprise. "Did we?"

"It was for deodorant, and there is no way you were sixteen at the time. I don't know when you started lying about your age, but it had to be after that, because we were supposed to be playing college students on a date." He narrowed his eyes, studying her. "How old are you *really*? Twenty-five? Twenty-six?"

Her lips pulled into a satisfied smirk. "Twenty-seven."

"You're only two years younger than me." He shook his head, marveling that she had the world convinced she was only twenty-two. "So when we did that interview last year, the woman I was talking to was twenty-six years old—not a teenager. Hardly dirty old man territory."

"Regardless of how old you may or may not have suspected I was, my character in the film we were talking about was sixteen. Every single person watching that inter-view saw a grown man commenting on a teenager's body. How do you think that makes teenage girls feel when they see a man reducing someone their age to body parts and a fitness regimen? It's bad enough when it happens to adult women. I mean, come on, I was nominated for an Oscar the year before, and all you wanted to talk to me about was how tight my costume was."

"You're absolutely right. It was shitty of me, and I apologize."

He could tell he'd surprised her by the way her mouth opened, all ready to argue with him. When his words sank in, she blinked at him and pressed her glossy pink lips together. Like she was annoyed he'd caved so easily.

"I'm glad you acknowledge it," she said finally, which wasn't exactly an acceptance of his apology, but he suspected it was as close as he'd get.

"Have you watched any of the interviews I've done in the last year?"

She let out a derisive huff. "No. Why would I?"

"If you had, you'd know I don't ask actresses those kinds of questions anymore."

"Really?" Kimberleigh's head swiveled toward him, her gaze narrowing in disbelief.

"Really. Even when their publicists feed them to me, I steer clear of that sort of questioning now."

"Because of me?"

"Yes. Because you were right to throw it in my face. It's an unfair double standard. When you pointed it out—live on national television—it was a needed wake-up call. I realized that wasn't the kind of interviewer I wanted to be."

"If you knew it was shitty, why did you do it in the first place?"

"You know why. Pressure to perform. The need to make a name for myself." He gave her a pointed look. "To get a good interview out of a subject who wasn't giving me a lot to work with."

She bristled. "Are you saying I asked for it?"

"No. That is absolutely not what I'm saying. But you had your back up from the moment you set foot in the studio that day. I don't know why, and it doesn't matter. But I could sense your resistance and it spooked me. When I started to feel the interview tanking, I got desperate and made a bad choice."

"You sure did."

"I'm not trying to excuse it. I'm simply explaining why it happened. I was still pretty new to the morning show segment at that point, and I felt like I had to prove myself. Before that I'd mostly done red carpet interviews and puff pieces that were more about regurgitating promotional talking points than getting under the surface of an interview subject to reveal something substantive and compelling."

She made a scoffing noise, as if she found the idea of Spencer doing anything substantive or compelling utterly absurd. "Asking me about my underwear is certainly one way of getting under my surface."

He cut a sideways look at her, resisting the urge to snipe back. "I know it's hard to believe, but I am not, in fact, perfect. I was still trying to find my feet with the morning show interviews at the time. I thought I was asking the questions the audience wanted answers to—and maybe I was—but after you humiliated me on-air, I decided I didn't want to pander to those kinds of interests anymore."

She gave him a look of disbelief. "*I* humiliated *you*?"

"Let's call it a mutual humiliation."

Her chin lifted stubbornly. "Which you instigated."

"Yes, I did. And I deserved what I got. But I also learned

from it and changed. I've stopped aiming for the low-hanging fruit."

"Like you did with Poppy Carpenter?"

He eyed Kimberleigh speculatively as something clicked into place. "Is that why you were so hostile with me from the get-go? Because you were pissed about my interview with Poppy Carpenter?"

"That interview was cruel and unprofessional."

"Maybe, but what happened with Poppy wasn't my fault." He'd taken a lot of flak for that interview and couldn't help getting defensive about it. "I'm willing to own my mistakes, but that wasn't one of them. Her publicist gave me those questions in advance. She led me to believe Poppy had approved them."

"Then why weren't they covered in the pre-interview?"

"Because Poppy was so late for the pre-interview we didn't have a chance to go over much of anything." She'd also been so hungover when she finally showed she'd barely been able to speak coherently, but Spencer kept that to himself. Because he actually did have principles and wasn't in the habit of telling tales out of school.

Kimberleigh regarded him with a frown as if she was assessing his honesty. Which, frankly, after everything he'd done and said tonight, pissed him off a little. Shouldn't he have earned himself at least some benefit of the doubt?

Meeting her gaze, he lifted a challenging eyebrow. "Believe me or don't. That's what happened. I wasn't trying to ambush her. I never would have broached a subject that sensitive without prior approval."

Kimberleigh's expression revealed nothing. If she believed him, he couldn't tell. "Are you saying Poppy actually okayed the questions? Or are you implying her publicist went behind her back?"

Spencer leaned his head against the wall. "I honestly don't know what happened. But that wasn't how I wanted that interview to go down."

"You didn't want all the attention it generated for you when it went viral?"

"Not like that. I don't want to become known as a bully who makes abuse victims cry. It's not great for getting interview subjects to open up to me."

"Hmm."

He looked over at Kimberleigh, whose expression was still infuriatingly unreadable. "Does that mean you believe me? Or do you still think I'm an asshole and a creep?"

"I don't think you're a creep." He could swear he saw a hint of a smile playing at the corner of her lips. Was it possible the ice queen was actually warming to him?

"That's an improvement from an hour ago, at least. I guess I'll take it as a win."

Kimberleigh shrugged. "The jury's still out on how much of an asshole you are, but your percentage has dropped somewhat." Her tone was dry but teasing, without the usual permafrost. And she was definitely smiling.

"From one hundred percent asshole to what? Ninety percent? Eighty?" He had to admit he was enjoying egging her on.

She pretended to consider it. "Let's say fifty."

"Only fifty percent asshole? Wow. I'm taking that as a huge compliment, considering the source."

"You should." Her smile grew, and Spencer felt that warm flare in his chest again.

Oh fuck. Oh no.

Just about the stupidest thing he could do right now would be to go and develop feelings for someone like Kimberleigh Cress.

And yet that was exactly what he seemed to be doing.

three

"DO you have a driver you need to call? Or can I order you a car?"

Kimberleigh shook her head. "I've got a room upstairs. I'll be fine." She just needed to get back to the suite, and then she could relax again.

Unfortunately getting to her suite required a long walk down a corridor potentially filled with people, an elevator ride, and another walk down another long hotel corridor. Her stomach churned at the prospect.

"Will you let me walk you there?" Spencer asked as though he could read her mind.

God, wasn't that a horrifying thought? Spencer Devlin having access to all her private thoughts and feelings.

Kimberleigh regarded him warily, surprising herself by actually considering the offer. Under normal circumstances she'd never let a man she barely knew accompany her to her hotel room alone. But these were not normal circumstances. Spencer had already seen her at her most vulnerable and been nothing but considerate and gentlemanly. And they were hardly strangers at this point. Over the last hour she felt like she'd gotten to know him a lot better. Even grown to like him, loath as she was to admit it.

Professionally, he was aggravating and potentially treacherous. But on a personal level, there was something intensely reassuring about his calm, understated competence.

But did she trust him?

Yes.

Maybe.

She wanted to, anyway. He seemed like a decent man. Or at least like he wanted to be a decent man. Experience had taught Kimberleigh not to let her guard down around anyone, but her instincts were trying to convince her Spencer was safe.

It was disconcerting. Usually she had no trouble keeping people at a distance. But for some reason she didn't want to push Spencer away right now. She'd liked having him close in her moment of need.

Too much, probably.

She had the odd feeling that she was standing on the threshold of one of the magical doorways from the *Otherwhere* movies that had shot her to stardom. The doors led you to a parallel universe where you'd made different choices that had each opened up a whole new life for an alternate version of you, every decision branching off from the ones before it, creating an infinite tree of possibilities. Whatever answer she gave Spencer, she couldn't shake the sense that this one small choice would ripple through her future in ways she couldn't predict.

But when she looked into his open, concerned expression, Kimberleigh knew she felt safer letting him escort her than she did venturing up to her room by herself.

"Okay," she told him, not entirely convinced it was the right decision. "I appreciate that."

He gave her an appraising once-over. "Are you ready to go now?"

Forcing a smile she didn't feel, Kimberleigh gave him a nod.

Spencer got to his feet and walked over to the double doors leading to the hotel corridor. He pushed one open wide enough to lean out and look around.

Her smile froze at the sudden influx of sound from outside. The ballroom was on the floor above the hotel lobby, facing onto a large atrium, and the roar of noise from below mingled with the music and conversation pouring out of the ballroom next door.

Spencer closed the door again, blessedly muting the noise for a moment, and gestured her over. "It looks pretty clear if we go to the right, away from the lobby. There's a bank of elevators at the end of the hall."

Nodding, Kimberleigh reached up to touch her hair, checking that it was still picture-perfect. They might run into press out there. Or fans with cameras.

Shit, what if she lost it again?

Spencer pushed the left door open and stepped out, holding it open for her. She girded herself and moved into the corridor, walking briskly past him as she made for the elevators.

He fell into step beside her, his posture casual as he spoke in a reassuring tone. "There are a lot of people behind us, mingling in the hall outside the ballroom, but they don't seem to be looking this way. Just keep walking and pretend we're deep in conversation about some very important business matter. People will be less likely to interrupt if they think we're doing business."

The steadiness of his voice helped keep her focused. The elevators were a ways away, but every step brought her closer to them and the promise of privacy once those big metal doors closed behind them.

"What sort of important business matters are we allegedly discussing?" she asked, trying to play along with the charade. "Are we trading stock tips? Comparing notes on our agencies? Or maybe you're offering to ghostwrite my autobiography."

His eyebrows lifted as he shot her a sideways grin. "Publishing an autobiography at twenty-two? Ambitious."

Halfway there now. One foot in front of the other. One step at a time. She could do this.

"Since we're pretending, I may as well aim high, don't you think?"

"In that case, I'm afraid I'll be too busy winning a Pulitzer to lend my considerable writing talents to your autobiography, intriguing as the project sounds."

She glanced at him in surprise. "A Pulitzer, really? I had no idea you harbored such lofty aspirations."

He gave her a shrug. "What's the saying? 'Shoot for the moon. Even if you miss you'll land among the stars.'"

They reached the elevators finally, and Kimberleigh punched the up button. Clenching her teeth, she looked at the lighted numbers above the two sets of doors to track the elevators' progress. They were both on the top floor and seemed to be in no hurry to come pick them up down on two. She peeked around Spencer and saw a cluster of people at the other end of the hall.

"You okay?"

"Fine." She took a deep breath and let it out again, trying to recall the way she'd matched her breathing to Spencer's earlier. The feel of his heart beating against her palm. His big warm hand covering hers. She still had his ring, and she clenched it tightly, trying to focus on the texture and weight of it like he'd told her to do.

Unexpectedly, Spencer's arm wrapped around her, tucking her against him and using his body to shield her from curious eyes. She would have taken offense at the presumption if she hadn't been so desperately grateful for it.

And somehow he'd known. He'd sensed exactly what she'd needed and offered it instinctively. It unnerved her to think she'd been so transparent.

He bent his head, and his breath tickled her ear. "I've got you. You're safe."

The heat radiating through his dress shirt chased away the shivers traveling down Kimberleigh's spine. She fought an overwhelming urge to snuggle against him, although she did allow herself to lean into him a little. He responded by tightening his arm around her.

Closing her eyes, she let the solidness of him surround her like a weighted blanket, using him as both a shield and a shelter. The scent of Spencer's skin, faintly perfumed by his cologne, made her feel dizzy. No, not dizzy—giddy. The good kind of lightheaded, not the bad kind she'd felt earlier. Her heart was thumping in her chest, but it wasn't racing like an impending panic attack. It was beating with excitement. Exhilaration.

It was an unfamiliar feeling. One she only vaguely remembered from her distant past. Another life. Another Kimberleigh.

She hadn't experienced anything like this in a long time, because she couldn't afford to let herself feel this way anymore. Especially not with Spencer Devlin.

What was she doing? He was the enemy.

You despise him, remember?

Except she didn't. Not anymore. She'd forgiven him for his mistakes. Reluctantly come to respect him even, for owning up to them so candidly.

But that didn't change the fact that their careers put them at odds. They could be professionally friendly, but that was all. She could never allow herself to forget that he wasn't on her side. His interests were not in her best interest and never would be.

She had no business letting Spencer hold her like this. And in public, no less. Imagine if they were seen like this. The way tongues would wag.

She should step back. Put some distance between them. Now.

But she couldn't. It had been too long since anyone had offered her this kind of physical comfort. Once she stepped away from Spencer, that would be the end of it. She'd never be this close to him again.

The elevator dinged its approach and he released her, doing what she couldn't. He shifted a safe distance away, protecting her dignity in case there was anyone on the elevator when the door opened.

To Kimberleigh's relief, the elevator was empty. She punched the button for her floor and leaned against the wall, letting out a long breath as the door closed behind them, temporarily shutting out the world.

"You okay?" Spencer stayed on his side of the elevator, making no move to get close to her again. It was for the best, but she found herself disconcertingly disappointed by it.

"I'm good." Refusing to look at him, she watched the numbers climb. As soon as the door opened, she rocketed out of the elevator, heading for her room as fast as her four-inch heels would take her.

Spencer ambled along behind her, not bothering to catch up to her now that they were alone—although she was acutely conscious that at any moment one of the doors on this floor could open and someone could see them together, walking toward her room. Kimberleigh quickened her steps, digging into her clutch for her room key as she covered the last few yards.

When she reached her door, she paused and turned to face him, clutching the key card in her hand. "This is where we say good night."

Sauntering to a stop a good six feet away from her, Spencer shoved his hands in his pockets. "Are you going to be okay on your own?"

"I'll be fine." She'd always been fine on her own. She didn't need to be taken care of. Not by anyone.

He nodded. "Get some rest. The adrenaline crash you're about to experience is no joke."

"Thank you...for everything." It wasn't enough to repay him for the kindness he'd shown, but it was all she could afford to give him.

"It was my genuine pleasure." His eyes lingered on her, his expression unexpectedly serious. For a second it looked like he was about to say something else, but then he just turned and walked away.

Kimberleigh unlocked her door with a trembling hand. As she pushed it open she looked down the hall and saw Spencer glance back over his shoulder, checking to make sure she got inside okay. Dragging her eyes away from him, she slipped inside the suite.

As the heavy door fell shut behind her with a loud *clunk*, she stumbled over to the couch and collapsed on top of it. She needed to get up and pry herself out of this motherflipping corset. Take her makeup off. Remove all the bobby pins from her hair.

Instead of doing any of those things, she stayed where she was, staring up at the ceiling and thinking about Spencer Devlin. The scent of his aftershave still clung to her skin and the memory of his smile lingered warmly in her chest.

She'd never expected to have a civil conversation with him, much less an actively enjoyable one.

Much less whatever that was she'd felt when he'd cuddled her at the elevators.

Crap.

Her breath stuck in her chest, and she pushed herself upright. That was when she realized she was still clutching his grandfather's ring in her hand.

Double crap.

four

"YOU SHOULD GO HOME," Spencer said as he set a takeout container on his assistant's desk. "It's Christmas Eve."

Vanessa looked up from her computer and yanked off her headphones. "Do you mean that? Because I'll go." Her eyebrows arched as her gaze fell on the takeout container. "Is that for me?"

"Don't I always bring you tiramisu from Cecconi's?" It was her favorite, and since she was the only thing keeping Spencer's life from falling completely apart, he tried to keep her very, very happy. "And yes, I mean it. Go home. Have a good Christmas."

"How was your lunch?" she asked, getting up to follow him into his office.

He grimaced as he shrugged out of his coat. "Tedious. But I was able to confirm my source's information. Carson Daly wants to move on from *Last Call* after his contract runs out."

"That's good, right? For you, anyway." Vanessa took his coat from him and hung it on the rack by the door.

"Potentially. It depends if the network decides to replace him or fill the slot with a new show. Either way, there may be an opportunity to throw my hat in the ring."

"I pulled together the research for your next two *Today Show* interviews in case you want to read it over the hiatus. It's in your email."

"Thanks." As he sank down in his chair, he noticed Vanessa giving him an odd look. "What?"

"Kimberleigh Cress's assistant called while you were at lunch."

Spencer froze as his heart tried to kick through his chest.

Kimberleigh.

The woman who had dominated his thoughts since their encounter. And not just because she still had his grandfather's ring. He hadn't been able to get her out of his head. He couldn't stop remembering the scent of her perfume and the feel of her hand in his. She'd already cost him two sleepless nights thanks to the marathon of fantasies his mind had insisted on conjuring.

Down, boy. She probably just wanted to arrange the return of his ring. That was all. No reason to go pinning his hopes on a long shot.

Forcing his shoulders to relax, he affected an air of casual curiosity as he glanced up at his assistant. "About?"

"She said, and I quote, 'Kimberleigh would like to speak with him at his earliest convenience.'"

"Did she happen to mention why?"

"No. I asked but she wouldn't say." Vanessa lifted an

inquisitive eyebrow. "I added the callback number to your contacts."

"Okay. Thanks."

"Do you want me to stay?" Vanessa offered, clearly dying to know why Spencer was suddenly getting a call from Kimberleigh Cress after being on her blacklist for a year.

"Nope." Spencer waved his assistant toward the door. "Take your tiramisu and make a run for it before I think of more work for you to do."

Vanessa arched a judgy eyebrow, not the least bit intimidated by his threat. "You're leaving soon too, right? You're not working late on Christmas Eve?"

"Don't worry. I just have a few things I want to do and then I'm out of here."

Spencer waited while Vanessa went back to her desk and packed up her things. After she'd called a final goodbye on her way out, he got up and closed his office door.

Then he called the number Vanessa had put in his phone.

"Hello?"

"Kimberleigh?" He recognized her voice immediately, although he hadn't expected her to answer the call herself. "It's Spencer Devlin."

"I have your ring," she said, not bothering with niceties or chitchat.

"Yes, you do."

"I'm sorry about that. I didn't mean to keep it."

"That's okay."

"I wasn't sure if you'd want me to messenger it back to you. I thought it might be special."

"It is."

45

"I could…" She paused and he held his breath. "We could meet somewhere. So I could give it back to you in person."

"Sure. That'd be fine." He tried not to sound as excited as he felt, because he had a feeling that might spook her, and then he'd end up getting the ring back from her assistant instead of getting to see Kimberleigh again. "When do you want to meet?"

"What about tonight?" she suggested unexpectedly.

"Tonight's Christmas Eve," he pointed out.

"Right." She sounded like she'd forgotten what day it was. "You've probably got plans."

"I don't, actually. Do you?"

"No. No plans."

Something squeezed in his chest at the thought of Kimberleigh spending Christmas Eve alone. Not that he'd been doing anything different. They were both in the same lonely boat apparently. "Then let's do it tonight. Where would you like to meet?"

There was the briefest of hesitations before she said, "I'd prefer not to go anywhere public, if that's all right."

"That's fine. I understand."

"I can bring it to your house. Or you can come to mine."

Spencer's heart gave a little jump of anticipation, and he told it to settle the fuck down. "Either's fine with me," he said to Kimberleigh. "Whichever you're more comfortable with."

"I don't want to put you to any trouble. I'm the one who rudely forgot to return it."

"It's no trouble. I can come to you if that's what you want."

"All right. Let's do that. Seven o'clock?"

"Sounds good."

"Is this your cell phone? I'll text you the address."

"Yes, perfect."

"I'll see you at seven."

"I'll be there."

He disconnected the call and stared at his phone, not really sure what they'd just arranged. Was she just going to hand him back his ring and say good night? Or was she hoping for something more?

Spencer was definitely hoping for something more.

Either way, he'd find out in approximately five hours.

five

KIMBERLEIGH LIVED IN BRENTWOOD, in a Mediterranean style house on a large, gated lot. When Spencer used the intercom at the end of the driveway, she answered herself and buzzed him in.

As he got out of his car, he nervously pushed his sleeves up. He'd spent entirely too long deliberating over his outfit for an encounter that could very well last only a few seconds. In the end, he'd gone casual with a thin crewneck sweater and a pair of soft, faded chinos.

Further deliberations had ensued over whether to show up empty-handed or with some kind of gift. Flowers were definitely over-the-top, but a bottle of wine might be seen as an acceptable peace offering under the circumstances. After considerable internal debate, he eventually decided to bring nothing but his authentic self. He didn't want to give the impression that he expected anything from her. Better to follow Kimberleigh's lead and let her tell him what she was willing to offer. If anything.

Getting close to Kimberleigh felt like trying to befriend a

porcupine. If you moved too suddenly or did the wrong thing, you were liable to get a snootful of quills. A smart man would shake off this frustrating infatuation, get his grandfather's ring back, and leave Kimberleigh Cress the hell alone.

Clearly Spencer was not a smart man, because when Kimberleigh opened the door, his heart stupidly tried to leap into his throat.

He'd never seen her looking so casual—or so beautiful. She wore lounge pants, a cozy pink sweater with a wide neck that hung loosely on her shoulders, and no makeup at all. She had freckles, he was delighted to discover. A light scattering of them dusted her nose and cheekbones like constellations. Her golden hair was pulled back in a sloppy bun and her feet were bare despite the chilly temperature.

This wasn't Kimberleigh Cress the burgeoning superstar who stood before him. It was the woman underneath all the glamour and pomp. The real Kimberleigh.

She was stunning.

"You made it." As greetings went, it wasn't the warmest he'd ever received, but coming from Kimberleigh it almost felt like a friendly hug.

He arched what he hoped was a playful eyebrow. "Did you doubt me?"

"Always." A slight twitch at the corner of her lips let him know she was teasing, which was a nice change from the active hostility that had dominated most of their previous interactions. She stepped back and gestured him inside. "Come in."

Her house smelled like flowers and vanilla. As he followed Kimberleigh into a spacious, high-ceilinged great room, he couldn't help noticing how nicely her gray lounge pants clung to her ass—and how nice her ass was.

A gas fire glowed in a large stone fireplace faced by a grouping of white couches and matching armchairs. The furnishings were stylish but cozy. Built-in shelves covered with books graced one whole wall of the open-plan dining area. He itched with curiosity to know her reading tastes, but Kimberleigh headed in the opposite direction, into a vaguely rustic, Italian-style kitchen.

"Do you want some wine? I just opened a bottle of red."

"I'd love some."

She got a glass down from a stem rack next to the wine fridge and filled it from an open bottle of pinot noir sitting out on the island. Passing the glass to him, she picked up her own half-filled wineglass. "Cheers."

"Cheers." Spencer clinked his glass against hers and they both drank. "This is nice." Spencer reached for the bottle to study the label. "Are you into wine?"

"Not really. I know what I like, but that's about it. Are you a wine person?"

He shook his head as he set the bottle down. "I can fake it well enough to pass in company, but it's all an illusion."

"That'd make a good title for your autobiography." Her eyes were bright and playful, and he couldn't help grinning in response.

"Ouch." He pressed a hand to his heart. "Harsh but accurate."

Kimberleigh's laughter twined around him, and he tried to remember if he'd ever heard her laugh before other than when she was playing a character.

"Oh, before I forget…" She dug into the pocket of her

lounge pants and produced his grandfather's ring. "Thank you for the loan. I'm sorry to have kept it." Her fingertips brushed his palm when she placed it in his hand, and something that felt like an electric current sizzled up his arm.

The gold was warm from her body heat, and he clenched his fist around it as he shoved it deep in his pocket. "Like I said the other night, it was my pleasure."

"The ring thing's a neat trick. Do you always carry it with you?"

He nodded. "It's a grounding technique I learned in therapy." It was on the tip of his tongue to ask if she'd ever sought therapy for her panic attacks, but he suspected that might be too intrusive. Instead he settled for a more benign "How are you?"

She gave him a speculative look. "Is that a polite inquiry as to my general well-being? Or are you asking if I've had any more panic attacks?"

"Have you?"

"No. Not since the one you witnessed on Saturday."

"I take it you made it home from the hotel all right."

"I did."

"I'm glad."

She arched an eyebrow. "Were you worried about me?"

"Of course I was."

"You don't need to do that."

"If only there was an on-off switch for basic human empathy," he deadpanned.

"There's not?" she replied just as dryly.

"Not for me there's not."

Her mouth quirked. "Don't tell me you're a big softie."

"I am, actually. And I've got my Soft Bro membership

card to prove it. It's a very competitive club. In order to qualify you have to help a dozen little old ladies across the street, volunteer to walk dogs at the local animal shelter, and kiss at least four babies a month."

When she laughed again, it sent a thrill of pleasure through him. He'd always been good at making people laugh, but Kimberleigh was a tougher audience than most. Every smile felt like an achievement, which made a laugh the equivalent of taking home the gold.

Her lashes lowered as she stroked a finger around the rim of her wineglass. "You really didn't have any plans tonight?"

"No. Other than working, probably, which I do most nights. What about you?"

She gave a light shrug as she sipped her wine. "I'm not big on holiday celebrations."

"Yeah, me neither." The words came out more bitter sounding than he intended.

Kimberleigh's gaze fixed on him, sharpening with interest. "Why not?"

His eyes flicked downward as he swirled his wineglass. "When I was growing up, holidays tended to be...unpleasant."

"How so?"

Talking about his childhood was something Spencer generally tried to avoid, but he didn't want Kimberleigh to feel like he was hiding anything. It seemed important to show her he was willing to be open. She'd unwittingly exposed some of her own vulnerability, and he didn't want her feeling like that put her at a disadvantage. Maybe by

52

sharing something painful and personal about himself, he could level the playing field between them.

But more than that even, he wanted her to know him. To understand him. Possibly even start to trust him.

He cleared his throat. "My parents drank even more than usual on holidays, which made the atmosphere in our house more volatile. Christmas especially, tended to be a stressor." He grimaced. "There aren't a lot of warm holiday memories in my past, so I've gotten in the habit of mostly ignoring them."

His parents had been functional alcoholics for the most part. They'd held down jobs, maintained friendships, kept Spencer fed and clothed when he was little. Most people who knew them probably wouldn't suspect they had a problem. Sometimes they'd go days or even weeks without incident, and during those peaceful stretches things had been fine. Happy, even. But eventually something would set one or the other of them off.

Alcohol had affected his parents differently. His mother was prone to violent rages—breaking things and lashing out physically—while his father retreated into quiet, calculated cruelty, inflicting pain with his words rather than his hands. Spencer supposed he'd been lucky that it hadn't been the other way around—although luck hadn't been something he'd felt he had much of back then.

"Do you still talk to your parents?" Kimberleigh asked in the same sympathetic yet penetrating tone Spencer used to delve into his interview subjects' painful pasts. He couldn't tell if she was actually interested or simply enjoying the chance to turn the tables on him.

"Not in years. When I left Valdosta, I left for good."

The last time he'd been in the same room with his parents, his father had told him not to bother coming back. He might not have meant it—his father said a lot of things when he was angry that he later tried to retract after he'd calmed down—but this time Spencer had taken him literally. He'd walked out of the house and hadn't spoken to either of his parents since.

"A Georgia boy." Kimberleigh's eyebrows lifted slightly as she studied him. "So that accent you occasionally drop into is real."

"Real as rain," he replied, letting his drawl come out. He mostly suppressed it when he was speaking on camera, but sometimes slipped into it when he was conversing informally. People seemed to find it disarming, which could be useful in certain situations. "Did you think it was a put-on?"

The corners of her lips tilted. "Possibly."

"I'll have you know this folksy charm is one hundred percent authentic."

"Aren't you just full of surprises?"

God, he wanted to touch her. Instead, he settled for watching as she took another sip of her wine. More like stared at her, really.

He wasn't used to this sort of infatuation. Usually he was able to be more circumspect when it came to his sex life. If a woman didn't return his interest right away or came with too many complications, he simply shifted his interest to someone else. He wasn't prone to crushes or the intrusive, obsessive feelings that came with them.

Whatever this was, it didn't feel like ordinary physical attraction. The pull Spencer felt toward Kimberleigh was much stronger. Gravitational, almost.

"What about you?" he asked when she set her wineglass down.

"What about me?"

"What's your beef with holidays?"

She raised one shoulder and let it fall. "More or less the same as yours."

"Your alcoholic parents forever ruined them for you?"

Her lips pressed together. "Not exactly."

When she didn't say anything else he frowned slightly. "You're not still worried I'm fishing for a scoop, are you? Because I promise you I'm not. Anything you say to me stays between us unless we both explicitly agree otherwise." He grabbed the bottom of his sweater like he was going to pull it up. "Do you want to check me for a wire?"

It won him another small laugh as she reached out to stop him from flashing his chest. "Not necessary." Her fingers lingered on his hand for a second, stroking lightly before she withdrew.

Once again, Spencer had felt something shock through him at the connection. He let go of his sweater, resisting the urge to rub the back of his hand, which glowed with warmth where Kimberleigh had touched him.

The smile faded from her lips as she turned her head to gaze at the darkness beyond the window, offering him her profile. "I grew up in foster care. Mostly in group homes. So I learned not to put too much store in holiday celebrations."

"You don't have any family?"

Their eyes met, and something that felt like recognition passed between them.

"No."

"What happened to your parents? If you don't mind my

asking."

"My dad was never in the picture. My mom died when I was eight." She lifted her wineglass to her lips.

He considered her for a moment. "When I was a kid I used to wonder what it would be like to be taken away by the state and put into foster care. I thought about it a lot, actually."

"It wasn't all bad. But the bad parts could be pretty bad." She dragged her teeth over her lower lip. "In an odd way, it was probably the best preparation I could have had for this career. It toughened me up and taught me how to watch my own back." Her voice was flat, but her expression cracked a little, betraying more than she probably wanted.

A rush of tender, protective feelings rose in him. She tried so hard to act strong, but all Spencer saw was how desolate and scarred she was underneath the hard outer shell.

He moved toward her instinctively, wanting to comfort her or…something. He couldn't help himself. He was a hugger by nature.

So he hugged her.

Kimberleigh stiffened in surprise as his arms wound around her. He half expected her to shove him away and throw her wine in his face. But then he felt her hands tentatively slide around his waist and settle on his back. Leaning into him, she rested her cheek against his chest. He imagined she was listening to his heartbeat.

"What are you doing to me?" she whispered.

"Hugging you. I thought that was obvious." He felt lighter with her in his arms. Like he could breathe easier. What was that even about?

"That's not what I meant and you know it."

He hadn't known any such thing. Not until she said it. He hadn't known for sure that she was feeling anything close to what he was.

Sliding a hand around the nape of her neck, he pulled back to look at her. Her eyes lifted, meeting his. He could feel her trembling. His thumb nestled under her chin, tipping it up.

He leaned in and kissed her cheek. Her forehead. Then finally her lips in the lightest of feather-soft touches before pulling back again.

They stared into each other's eyes, breathing together. Spencer held himself very still, waiting to see what Kimberleigh would do.

When she arched toward him, he met her halfway. Her lips parted as they slid against his, and he matched her stroke for stroke. She tasted rich and spicy like the wine they'd been drinking, but with more sweetness.

His hand slid along her jaw as he kissed her more deeply, humming his pleasure into her mouth. Her hands curled into his back, and she pressed herself against him. Searching. Straining. Demanding.

As he trailed kisses along her jaw to her ear then down her throat, her fingers slipped under his shirt. The touch of her hands on his bare skin sent a shudder through him. His mouth found its way back to her mouth, delving deep as her fingernails dragged over his stomach.

But when she started to tug at the button of his pants, he captured her hands and pulled back to give her a questioning look. "Two days ago you hated my guts."

Her lashes fluttered, her breathing as ragged as his.

"And?"

"I'm not into hate fucks. No judgment if you are, but it's really not my thing. So if that's what this is—"

"It's not."

He scanned her face, trying to read her expression. "What is it, then?"

"Something else." She made an impatient noise. "Do I have to write you a sonnet to get in your pants?"

He grinned. "I'll never say no to a sonnet." When she rolled her eyes, he lowered his lips to her ear. "But I'll settle for hearing you say that you want me."

"I want you." Her hand closed over his, sliding it down to her breast. "Is that clear enough for you?"

Hearing her say the words ignited something inside him. His mouth slanted over hers hungrily as his hands roamed freely over her body, stroking, caressing, and exploring. She wasn't wearing a bra under her sweater, and she made a lovely, needy sound when he squeezed her nipple between his thumb and forefinger.

He couldn't get enough of kissing her. Touching her. Tasting her. His pulse drummed in his ears, quickening to a crescendo when she stroked him through his pants. Groaning, he gripped her ass and dragged her against him as his thigh pressed between her legs.

The hard edge of the marble counter dug into his hip, drawing his attention to the cold, inhospitable surfaces that surrounded them in their present location. He broke free of her lips and cupped her face, running his thumb along her jaw. "Living room or bedroom? Your choice."

She blinked at him, her eyes beautifully unfocused. "Bedroom. Definitely."

six

SPENCER GRINNED DOWN AT HER. "Lead on, Ponce de León."

God, he was so fucking corny. It shouldn't be sexy, yet somehow she found it completely irresistible. Folksy charm, indeed.

Am I really doing this? Kimberleigh asked herself as she tugged on his hand.

Yes, she definitely was. It might be the biggest mistake of her life, but there was no way she was turning back now. Not until she'd felt Spencer Devlin between her thighs.

She backed toward the stairs, pulling him along behind her. He only had eyes for her as she led him through the house and up to her bedroom.

As she dragged him toward the bed, she tugged him closer and grabbed the hem of his sweater, trying to push it up and off him. He obligingly yanked it over his head, then helped with the removal of hers.

His eyes drank her in with an intensity that filled her stomach with butterflies.

Ridiculous.

She'd been gazed at by so many lustful eyes at this point it shouldn't have the power to affect her anymore. It usually didn't. But something about the way Spencer looked at her made her feel seen on a whole other level than she was used to.

He lowered his head to trail his mouth over her breasts. As he circled his tongue around her nipple, Kimberleigh stroked her hands up his arms and over the wide expanse of his chest, appreciating the dusting of fine golden hair. It made a nice change from all the waxed male chests she usually encountered.

When he hooked an arm behind her knees and swept her off the floor, she made a noise of surprise. His mouth sought hers again as he laid her on the bed and pressed his weight into her. She skimmed her hands up his back, over his smooth, warm skin and taut muscles, loving the feel of him on top of her. It made her feel safe. Grounded. Like his body was a shelter she could hide herself in.

His fingers found the waistband of her lounge pants and he slid them down her legs, exposing the sheer pink thong she wore underneath—the one she was loath to admit she'd put on just for him, hoping he'd see it. Hoping he'd like what he saw.

A smile played on his lips as he slid a palm up her thigh, his eyes heating as he watched himself touching her. Her breath caught as he neared the thin band of elastic on her hip, and her leg twitched in impatient anticipation.

Lifting his gaze to her face, Spencer smoothed his hand over the barely-there triangle of lace covering her cleft and pushed her legs apart. When he shoved aside the tiny scrap of fabric and his fingers grazed her wet, aching center, Kimberleigh arched into him with an embarrassing whimper.

"You look so beautiful like this." His eyes were intent as he watched her react to his touch. Studying her. Making sure she liked it.

She did. *God*, she liked it so much. Her whole body sang as he caressed her. She moaned when he slipped a finger inside her. Jerked every time his thumb brushed her swollen clit. Quivered as pleasure rippled through her, driving her closer to the edge and then over it.

Just that quickly she was coming beneath him, surprising herself as she clenched around his fingers and bit down on her lip to keep from crying out his name.

She never came that fast. *Never.*

"My god." His voice was rough and raspy. "I could watch you do that all night long."

"Fine with me," she murmured when she could speak again.

He lowered himself over her, the hard planes of his body pressing her into the comforter as he kissed her. Slowly, softly. Like he was savoring her. Then harder, hungrier. Awakening a fresh pulse of desire between her thighs.

Inexplicably, he was still wearing pants. She could feel the hard length of his erection against her leg, but she couldn't reach it and she really needed to touch him. Wriggling against him, she managed to get her hands between them to unfasten his pants. When he realized what she was doing, he helpfully lifted his hips, allowing her better access.

"Fuuuuuck," he groaned when she wrapped her hand

around his cock. His hips jerked, pressing into her grip as she stroked him. "You're going to ruin me."

"These pants need to come off if I'm going to do it properly."

Wrenching himself away from her, he shoved his pants and underwear down. She sat up on her elbows, admiring the sight of his swollen, heavy dick, the patch of thick blond curls between his legs, the firm muscles of his thighs.

Impatient to feel him inside her, she pushed at her soaking wet thong, shimmying it down her hips. Licking his lips, he dragged it off her legs for her before crawling back onto the bed. His mouth was all over her, his body vibrating with tension as he pushed her back into the mattress. She tried to get her hand around his cock, but he caught her wrist and pinned it above her head as he sucked at her throat.

"Did you bring a condom?" she asked, arching into him.

He lifted his head with an expression of alarm. "No. Please tell me you've got some. Preferably within easy reach of the bed."

"You didn't bring one?"

His smile looked almost shy. "I didn't want to make assumptions."

"I invited you over to my house alone at night." Surely he wasn't that naive.

"Yeah, but I thought you hated my guts. It may surprise you to hear this, but you're not the easiest woman in the world to read."

She stroked her hand over his chest, pausing when she found his heartbeat. "I don't hate you."

He smiled against her lips as he kissed her. "I'm glad to hear it."

"Bottom drawer of the nightstand." She tilted her head to the left. "That one."

When he rolled away from her, the loss of his body left her shivering. But he wasted no time finding a condom and rolling it on. He was back almost immediately, warming her again in a slide of bare skin. She reached for his face, and he lavished her with kisses so hot and searing they felt like brands on her soul.

He shifted, repositioning himself, and she felt his length slide against her aching entrance. Teasing her. Torturing her. Driving her wild. "I want you," he breathed. "So fucking bad."

Breathless and shuddering with need, she arched toward him, straining for more friction. She was losing control and she didn't care anymore. "I want—" Her voice broke, desperation becoming agony. "I need—"

"What do you need?" He kissed her again, softly. "Tell me and it's yours. Anything you want."

"You," she growled. "I need to feel you inside me."

He entered her with a deft thrust of his hips, drawing a gasp from her as he stretched her sensitive flesh.

"Okay?" he murmured, holding himself still as he nuzzled a kiss against her temple.

It was better than okay. It was glorious, the way he filled her up with the most delicious pressure, turning her to liquid from the inside out. Nothing had ever felt this good.

"Spencer." She tangled her fingers in his hair and brushed her lips against his ear. "I want you to fuck me until I can't remember my own name."

He made an inhuman sound and jerked his hips, driving even deeper inside her. "Holy shit. You're perfect."

She sank her nails into his shoulder, urging him on with breathless moans as he thrust into her at just the right angle. Harder and faster. Finding the perfect rhythm.

"You feel so good," he groaned when she clenched her walls around him. "You're amazing. So beautiful."

Her senses narrowed until she was oblivious to everything but the press of his body, the scent of his sweat-slick skin, and the exquisite friction building where he stroked deep inside her, finding that shivery, tender spot that threatened to break her apart.

Fuck, she wanted more of that. She grabbed his ass with both hands, mindlessly grinding their hips together. Her gasps began to resemble sobs as the swirling pressure inside her built. Distantly, she was aware of him murmuring her name, telling her how gorgeous she was, urging her to fall apart for him and promising he'd be there to catch her.

A cry that might have been Spencer's name choked out of her as colors splashed across her vision. She clung to him, the only solid, tangible thing she could hold on to as the wave broke over her and she lost herself to more than just the sensation.

A HALF HOUR LATER, THEY WERE STILL IN KIMBERLEIGH'S bed. Still naked. Their bodies still tangled together. One might even say they were cuddling.

Ugh. Who even was she right now?

She should be herding him out the door, not blithely

nuzzling her face into his neck. Spencer's dick had obviously put some kind of enchantment on her. That was the only possible explanation.

Except it wasn't that. Whatever spell this was, it had been cast long before she got anywhere near his penis.

Kimberleigh had assumed this was just some inconvenient but temporary physical attraction. The freak result of pheromones and chemistry and whatever ineffable force ruled sexual urges. Thirst gone wild. Something she could get out of her system so she could move on with her life the way she usually did.

Unfortunately, banging it out didn't seem to have solved the problem. Au contraire. Sleeping with Spencer had made everything worse. Her feelings were snowballing seriously out of control. The addition of intimacy had only intensified her attraction and induced a complicating case of affection.

Affection. Ugh.

That was the problem right there. She actually *liked* him. She liked talking to him and listening to him talk. She liked the way he listened to her. The way he looked at her. The way she felt when he held her in his arms.

There was no denying it. She wanted Spencer around. As much as possible. For more than just sex.

You have bewitched me, body and soul.

Except this wasn't her favorite Jane Austen movie. This was her goddamn life.

"I can feel you thinking," Spencer murmured, stroking a hand over her head. "Anything you want to share with the class?"

Kimberleigh shook her head. "Just that I don't know what's come over me."

"Me."

She lifted her head and felt a dizzying, reckless punch of tenderness when their eyes met and he broke into a grin.

"Literally. I came on top of you a little while ago. You remember that, right?"

"That's not what I mean." She tried to sound irritated, but couldn't help smiling at his corny joke. She hated how much she adored his corny jokes.

He stroked his thumb over her cheek, his expression fading to seriousness. "I know."

"Post-coital cuddling isn't usually my style."

"Do you want me to leave?"

She should probably say yes, but that would be a lie. For once, she felt like telling the truth. So she did. "No."

He arched an eyebrow, apparently sensing her hesitation. "Sure about that?"

"Yes." What she wanted right now, more than anything, was to fall asleep in Spencer's arms and wake up to his gorgeous face in the morning.

His smile socked her right in the chest. "Maybe you just haven't found the right cuddling partner to realize your true cuddling potential."

"You think you're the right cuddling partner?"

"I am the *perfect* cuddling partner. Five-star ratings across the board. Cuddling is one of my many superpowers."

She tried and failed to stifle a laugh. "Modesty, thy name is Spencer Devlin."

His eyes crinkled with delight. "Did you just snort? Was that a snort-laugh?"

"It was a snort of derision."

"Kimberleigh Cress snorts when she laughs. I love it."

"Don't make fun." She tried to tweak his nipple, but he caught her hand and trapped it against his chest before it could do any damage.

"I'm not making fun." His thumb traced the curve of her lower lip. "I love that you snort when you laugh. My new life goal is to make you snort-laugh as much as possible."

What was she supposed to say to that? What was she supposed to do with a man who simply wanted to make her laugh?

Keep him.

She leaned in for a kiss and he met her halfway, his hand twisting in her hair as his lips softly, warmly caressed hers. A glowy feeling of contentment bloomed in her chest, and she gave up trying to fight it.

"Alexa, turn off the bedroom lights." As the room plunged into darkness, Kimberleigh stroked her hand over Spencer's chest until she found his heartbeat.

His arms tightened around her, and he pressed a kiss to her forehead. "Merry Christmas, Kimberleigh."

She snuggled closer and closed her eyes. "Go to sleep, Spencer."

seven

SPENCER AWOKE the next morning to the sound of an unreasonably loud and irritating dog yapping somewhere in the distance. As his eyes came into focus, he blinked at the unfamiliar surroundings and breathed in the scent of flowers and vanilla.

Kimberleigh's house.

He was in Kimberleigh's bed. That meant the soft, warm weight on his chest was Kimberleigh, still sound asleep and curled around him.

He couldn't imagine anything better to wake up to—annoying yappy dogs aside. Judging by the light pouring in the French doors, it was maybe an hour past sunrise. It was also Christmas Day, he remembered, which meant he didn't have to be anywhere other than right here.

Good. Because he was pretty happy to be here and in no hurry for the moment to end.

Spencer closed his eyes and tried to fall back asleep, but his bladder had its own agenda. After several uncomfortable minutes he finally gave up and managed to roll Kimberleigh off him without waking her.

Once he'd completed his business in the bathroom and helped himself to some mouthwash, he wandered back into the bedroom. Kimberleigh was still sleeping and exhibited no signs of waking up soon. Snagging his phone from the floor where it had fallen when he'd kicked off his pants last night, he crawled back into bed.

An hour later, he'd responded to a dozen emails, checked all the major entertainment news sites, and was halfway through the *New York Times* crossword when Kimberleigh finally began to stir beside him. She'd rolled back toward him in her sleep and pressed her face up against his side. One of her arms had curled around his thigh, hugging it like a teddy bear, which he found incredibly endearing. But as she came slowly awake, her hand flexed and slid up his leg. *All* the way up his leg.

Her eyes flew open, blinking against the morning glare a few times before they focused on his face. "Hi."

Spencer smiled down at her. "Good morning."

"You're still here," she mumbled in a groggy, sleep-roughened voice that made it difficult to tell whether she considered his presence a good thing or a bad thing.

"I am." If she was disconcerted to find him in her bed, she was really going to be taken aback when she noticed where her hand was.

Her brow furrowed. "Is my hand on your dick?"

"It is, yes." His now semi-hard dick that was getting harder by the second.

"Oh." There was a long pause. "Should I move it?"

"That depends what you're proposing to move and how."

Her smile warmed him like sunlight. "My hand. Would you like me to remove my hand from your dick?"

"I leave it entirely in your hands, so to speak. I'm fine with it where it is."

"Yes, I can feel that you are." Her fingers flexed, and he bit down on his lip to suppress a groan. "Are you working?" she asked, noticing the phone in his hand.

"Just entertaining myself while I waited for you to rouse from your coma." He tossed his phone onto the bed and stroked his hand over her back. "Did you sleep well?"

"I slept amazingly well." Her nose wrinkled. "I think I might have drooled on you a little. Sorry."

"A little drool never hurt anyone."

"I don't usually sleep well with someone else in the bed."

"I told you last night, I'm the perfect cuddling partner."

"You did." Something flashed across her expression, causing the smile to fade from her lips. Her gaze slid away from his and she took her hand off him, which was disappointing for a number of reasons.

When he couldn't stand the silence anymore, Spencer cleared his throat. "Not to ruin the romance of the moment, but do we need to talk about...?" He gestured between them. "You know. Us. This. Whatever."

Kimberleigh rolled away from him and stretched her arms over her head. "Do we?" There was an edge of something in her voice he didn't like. Annoyance, maybe. Or guardedness.

Shit.

He inhaled a long breath before he said, "It's just that I

can't decide if I should offer to make you coffee or if you're about to hand me my shoes and ask me to leave."

"I don't know where your shoes are, but you should probably put on pants before going outside." Her tone was breezy, but she still wasn't looking at him.

"All jokes aside," he said quietly.

She arched a wry eyebrow at him. "Oh? Now you want to be serious?"

His mouth twitched into a half-hearted smile. "Not that I don't enjoy our whip-smart banter."

"But you want to know if this is a one-and-done kind of deal," she said flatly.

He nodded. "Or if you envision it leading to something...more."

Please say more. Please say more.

"What do *you* want?" Her eyes were fully focused on him now.

He held her gaze and answered without hesitation. "I'd like it to be something more, but only if the feeling's mutual. I know how to exit gracefully when a graceful exit is requested."

Something flickered in the green depths of her eyes, and he died a million deaths trying to interpret it before she finally said, "I don't want you to exit."

They were the words he'd been hoping to hear, but the tone of her voice and the look on her face forestalled his celebratory fist-pump.

"But...?" he prompted, bracing himself.

"You should know up front that I don't do relationships."

"That's funny, because I distinctly remember reporting on several of your relationships."

Over the three years that he'd been doing red carpet interviews, Spencer had watched Kimberleigh parade multiple boyfriends through the press line. Her most recent relationship had ended just a couple of months ago, in fact, amidst a firestorm of media coverage after her actor boyfriend was photographed canoodling with an up-and-coming pop starlet. Spencer had even interviewed the guy earlier in the year, and he'd gone on at length about how happy and in love he and Kimberleigh had been.

If she was still getting over the breakup and wary of starting anything new, that was one thing. But she could at least say that instead of feeding him an obvious lie.

She bit down on her lip as her gaze flicked to his. "This stays between us?"

"Of course."

"Those relationships were all publicity stunts."

"All of them?" Spencer was well aware that fauxmances and "love contracts" happened all the time in Hollywood. They were an easy way of generating hype, either to promote a new project or distract from bad publicity. But Kimberleigh had been linked with a steady stream of romantic partners over the last four years on her rise to stardom. That was a lot of fake boyfriends and a lot of pretending.

"Every one you heard about." She tugged the sheet up over her chest as she rolled toward him onto her side. "The only way to protect my privacy is to create a fiction to offer up for public consumption. I give people what they want: a boyfriend they can talk about, judge, insult, fixate

72

their jealousy on, and tear to shreds. Someone who's used to the attention, knows exactly what they're in for, and is getting something out of it in return. Someone I don't have any feelings for, so the awful things people say can't hurt us."

There was a slight roughness to her voice that betrayed echoes of old pain. Clearly she'd had some bad experiences that had caused her to put up defenses around herself. What Spencer didn't know was how ironclad those defenses were and whether she was willing to let him inside.

He turned onto his side so they were face-to-face. "Okay. So...what? Other than these fake boyfriends, you just don't date? Like...at all? Is that what you're saying?"

Kimberleigh reached for his hand and curled her fingers around his. "I'm not willing to live my personal life in public. That means the things I care about have to stay private." Her thumb rubbed over his. "If we were to keep seeing each other, no one could know."

His mind faltered and got stuck on *I care*. Did that mean he was one of the things she cared about? Was that what she'd just said? His heart rocketed in his chest, but he only allowed himself to show a small smile. "Did you think I'd have a problem with that?"

"Some people do."

"I don't want to date you to raise my profile." He brought her hand to his lips. "I like you, and I want to spend time with you. If you want us to keep it to ourselves, I'm fine with that."

"It's not easy. Trust me."

He shrugged. "Katie Holmes and Jamie Foxx kept their relationship secret for five years."

"The thing is, you're the person people like me usually try to keep our secret relationships secret from."

"Are you suggesting I'd blow the lid on my own secret relationship? Because I'm a lot more invested in seeing you again than I am in reporting on your love life. Your romantic exploits are considerably more interesting to me on a personal level than a professional one."

"Right now, maybe. But what if things don't work out? What if I piss you off?"

"Am I going to seek revenge by writing a tell-all about our relationship, you mean?"

Her lips pressed into an unhappy line. "I suppose that's what I'm worried about, yes."

"Look, I told you that anything between us stays between us unless we both explicitly agree otherwise."

"I know."

He reached out to brush a strand of golden hair off her face, tucking it behind her ear. "So I guess it comes down to whether you're willing to trust me or not."

"I want to."

His palm cradled her jaw as his thumb traced the frown line around her lips. "But it's not easy for you. I know."

"It's not. Historically, I'm pretty much the worst at relationships."

"I don't know you that well yet—although that's something I'd very much like to change—but from what you have told me it doesn't sound like you've had many opportunities to practice." She lowered her eyes, but he tipped her chin up until she met his gaze again. "I can be patient. All I'm asking is that you try. At least give it a chance."

Kimberleigh's teeth scraped over her lower lip before she gave him a brief nod.

"Is that a yes?" he asked hopefully.

"It's a yes. Let's try."

"Good." Spencer rolled them both on the bed so he was lying on top of her. He nuzzled into her neck, letting some of his weight press her into the mattress as his cock hardened against her. "Now that we've dispensed with that, I have a very important question to ask you."

She angled her head, giving him better access to the soft skin of her throat as her hips tilted invitingly beneath him. "Ask away."

Moving lower, he cupped her breast and rubbed his stubble lightly over her nipple, enjoying the way it made her squirm against him. "Do you want coffee first and then sex? Or sex before I get up and make you coffee?"

Her fingers tangled possessively in his hair. "Definitely sex first. Then coffee. Then more sex."

It was the perfect answer. He couldn't think of a better way to start his day.

eight

"KIMBERLEIGH! Over here! Let's see a smile! Have you talked to Aidan since the breakup? How do you feel about his new girlfriend?"

Kimberleigh rested her hand on her hip, ignoring the cajoling voices trying to provoke a response as she posed on the Golden Globes red carpet. Her camera-perfect smile—not too wide with just a hint of teeth—never wavered as she pivoted, showing off her gown from every angle.

Once she'd done her time in front of the blinding array of camera flashes, she rejoined Stacie, who escorted her through the throng of celebrities and their handlers mingling in the arrivals area.

"First up is Spencer Devlin for *Hot Hollywood Nights*." Stacie leaned in close as she guided Kimberleigh around the massive train on Lady Gaga's poufy lavender gown. "I assume you're still okay with talking to him?"

Kimberleigh nodded, returning the waves of several people she knew. "It's fine."

She'd given her publicity team the okay to un-blacklist

Spencer. Tonight's red carpet interview would be their first on-camera interaction since the infamous interview a year ago.

It would also be their first time interacting in public since they'd begun sleeping together.

Or whatever it was they were doing. It definitely felt like more than just sex. But could you call it dating if you weren't actually going out on dates? Unless late-night rendezvous at her house counted as dates.

They'd been seeing as much of each other as possible given both their busy schedules and workaholic tendencies. She'd never realized how hard Spencer worked and how many irons he had in the fire. Most days he was up before dawn and going nonstop until nine or ten at night. Meanwhile, despite this being one of Kimberleigh's rare periods of "downtime" between projects, she was already in training for her next film, attending stunt rehearsals for an upcoming *Otherwhere* reshoot, and jammed up with meetings about potential future projects. All of which meant she didn't get to see nearly as much of Spencer as she would have liked.

She could see him now, however, up on the small platform the network had set up for him to conduct his red carpet interviews. He looked devastatingly handsome in his tuxedo as he stood under the bright lights talking to Sandra Oh.

Why had Kimberleigh never noticed how attractive he was before? Or the way his eyes twinkled when he smiled? She'd never really looked at him at all, to be honest. The only thing she'd seen was his job. The microphone he held in her face. The cameras pointed in her direction. The questions she was expected to navigate with grace and caution.

Spencer said something that caused Sandra Oh to clutch her stomach and let out a peal of laughter. Kimberleigh smiled, imagining the sort of sweet, dorky quip he'd probably just made. He really was amazingly good at his job. She'd scoffed when he'd called himself likable, but it was true. He had an uncanny knack for disarming people and getting them to open up to him.

Even Kimberleigh.

"Hey, hot stuff! You're looking fine as shit."

Smiling, Kimberleigh turned around to greet Poppy Carpenter. "Back at you, gorgeous. Love your hair that color."

Poppy leaned in for a delicate hug, mindful of their elaborate hair and makeup. "God, I feel like I haven't seen you in forever. Things have been so crazy, I barely know what city I'm in anymore. But I guess you've been pretty busy too, huh?"

"Yeah, I just got back from four months in London followed by a worldwide press tour. Are you in town for a while?"

"A couple of months, thank god, then I'm off to New Orleans. Get this"—she broke into a grin—"I'm doing a Joe Lincoln picture with Scotty Deacon."

Kimberleigh's eyebrows shot up in surprise. "Scotty's working again?"

Scotty was Robbie Scarborough's former best friend—the same one Poppy was rumored to have cheated on Robbie with while they were engaged. Kimberleigh was surprised to hear Poppy and Scotty were working together, considering Scotty had pretty much dropped off the map a few years ago after his substance abuse issues blew up his career.

Poppy nodded. "Yeah, he's two years sober and back at it."

"That's really great," Kimberleigh said, remembering that Poppy had once confided that she was scared Scotty wouldn't live to see his thirtieth birthday if he didn't get himself into rehab. "I'm so glad."

"Yeah, me too. I'm really proud of him."

"Kimberleigh, you're up in one minute," Stacie interjected.

Poppy smiled. "I better jet. But hey, I'm proud of you too. I mean damn, look how far you've come from playing my bratty kid sister."

"You're doing pretty well yourself. We've both come a long way."

"Hell yeah we have." Poppy's gaze flicked toward Spencer, who'd finished his interview with Sandra Oh and was conferring with a member of his crew. "Watch your back up there."

Spencer glanced their way, as if he could feel them talking about him. Kimberleigh's stomach dropped as his eyes met hers, but she kept her expression carefully neutral.

Poppy smiled and gave him a cheerful wave. "What a dick."

"We need to catch up," Kimberleigh said as she hugged Poppy goodbye. "Let's get together soon." She wanted to hear more about Scotty, but she was also curious to get Poppy's take on Spencer and that infamous interview. To compare her version of the story with his.

"Totally." Poppy released her and slipped back into the

crowd as one of Spencer's production crew gave Stacie a signal.

Kimberleigh was helped up the steps onto the small platform, where she found herself standing next to Spencer under an array of blinding lights. Quite close to him, in fact, since the platform wasn't very large. Close enough that she could smell his cologne and see the line behind his ear where his foundation hadn't been blended enough.

He greeted her with a distracted nod and touched his earpiece, all polite efficiency as he listened to his producer's instructions. "You ready?" he asked, finally giving Kimberleigh his full attention.

She nodded, suppressing a shiver as his gaze traveled over her and the corner of his mouth twitched in appreciation. He dragged his eyes away from her, rolling his shoulders as a crew member counted them off. The second they went live Spencer slipped into his charming on-camera persona as smoothly as flicking a switch.

"I'm here with the talented, lovely, and all-around wonderful Kimberleigh Cress, who's presenting tonight. Kimberleigh, you look absolutely stunning."

For a second, the full force of his smile rendered her motionless. Then she remembered she was on camera and actually expected to talk and behave like a functioning human being. And a glamorous, engaging one at that.

Following his lead, she adopted the pleasant and slightly flirty demeanor she reserved for public appearances. "Thank you so much, Spencer. Aren't you sweet?" She gifted him with a smile as she briefly touched his arm.

"Now, this is not your first time on this red carpet. You were nominated for a film called *Burning Down* two years ago. And you were only nineteen when you made that film, correct?"

"That's right, I was." Her smile warmed into something more genuine. Although she knew it was standard red carpet practice to mention previous nominations, the fact that he'd raised the subject of her work rather than dwelling on her looks meant he'd taken her complaints about their last interview to heart.

"Incredible. And tonight is your second time here as a presenter since then. So you're a total pro at this red carpet stuff now."

She let out a self-deprecating laugh. "Yes, that's me. Sure."

"Now, just between us, tell me the truth. Do you get nervous about presenting? You can be honest. I promise not to tell anyone." He winked, flashing a dimpled grin at the camera.

She played along with the gag, leaning in and gesturing him closer as if she were about to divulge a secret. "Is this a safe space?" she asked with an innocent flutter of her eyelashes.

"Absolutely. Safe as houses." His eyes twinkled as he bent toward her, so close she could feel his body heat warming her skin. "It's just you and me here. A couple of friends sharing secrets."

It was only a silly bit they were doing, but it felt ludicrously real. Spencer's manner was so beguiling, it was easy to forget the camera was even there—not to mention the production crew only a few steps away and the noisy red carpet throng surrounding them. His dazzling smile drew her in, and his eyes held her in their magnetic grip until the rest of the world seemed to melt away. She frequently felt something similar when they were alone together, but it was even more extraordinary given their current circumstances.

He really was disgustingly good at his job. And though his charisma was a superpower that could easily be abused, he seemed to take his professionalism more seriously than she'd previously allowed. People new to the spotlight or anxious being questioned on live TV probably found his presence deeply comforting—just like she had when he'd talked her through her panic attack.

"Well, the truth is…" Kimberleigh leaned into the mic Spencer held. "It's terrifying. I'm absolutely petrified the whole time I'm up there."

"Really?" He adopted an expression of surprised disbelief.

"Of course! There are—how many people watching the broadcast?"

"Nineteen million," he supplied automatically.

"Right, no big deal. Only nineteen million people watching you live." She tossed the camera a sardonic look worthy of *The Office*. "Plus, you know, when you're present-ing, there's all this added pressure because it's someone else's big moment—a moment they'll remember for the rest of their lives—so you don't want to get their name wrong or drop the statuette on their foot and ruin it for them in front of the whole world."

Spencer's eyes crinkled as he let out a throaty laugh. "Drop the statuette on their foot? Is that really something you're afraid of?"

"God yes! It keeps me up at night." She held her hand

out with her palm facing down. "Look at me, I'm getting a little shaky right now just talking about it."

"I never would have guessed. You're excellent at hiding it." Spencer's smile turned teasing. "And don't worry, when you're standing up there onstage tonight, we definitely won't all be waiting for you to drop the award on someone's foot."

She laughed along with the joke before turning it around on him. "What about you, Spencer? Do you ever get nervous to have so many people out there watching you on TV?" It wasn't something she'd ever asked him before, and she was honestly curious.

"Are you kidding? I'm a wreck right now." He tugged at the collar of his shirt. "I may look calm and collected on the outside, but inside I'm just a big ball of nausea."

She didn't believe that for a second. "Oh come on. I think you're just saying that to make me feel better."

"I promise you I'm not." As his gaze rested on her, his smile softened into something that looked startlingly like sincerity before he snapped back into professional mode again. "Now, Kimberleigh, I can't let you go without asking you about the next *Otherwhere* movie. The second one just came out last month and *wow*—I don't want to spoil anyone, but that ending! People are losing their minds. What can you tell us about the third one to tide us over until next December?"

She smiled demurely and made a zipping motion across her lips. "Not a thing."

"Come on now. This is our safe space, remember? You've gotta give me something."

Motioning for him to lean in again, she batted her

eyelashes and said, "I can confirm that I'm in the film. Does that help?"

"You're killing me, Kimberleigh." He'd said the exact same thing in his bed last night, and her chest flushed at the memory despite the chilly January temperature. Spencer's eyebrow arched slightly, as if he were remembering the same thing, before he turned back to the camera to wrap up the interview.

When they were off the air, he turned back to her and presented his hand for a businesslike shake. "Thank you for speaking with me. It was a real pleasure."

"Likewise," she murmured as she squeezed his hand, just that brief skin-to-skin contact melting her insides like fondue chocolate.

"This way, Kimberleigh. Watch your step." One of the crew offered her a hand down the steps, and she turned her back on Spencer and let herself be led away.

Stacie was waiting for her, looking pleased. "That was terrific. Do you feel good about it?"

"Yeah, it wasn't too bad." Kimberleigh lifted her eyes and found Spencer watching her with a subtle smile on his face.

"You absolutely killed it," Stacie said. "You two have amazing chemistry."

"I guess we do." Kimberleigh smiled to herself as Stacie guided her to her next red carpet interview. "Go figure."

nine

SPENCER SHUFFLED his feet impatiently as he stood on Kimberleigh's doorstep holding a grocery bag. He'd worked last night and all day today, which meant he hadn't seen her in…thirty-nine hours and twenty-four minutes. But now he was here and only seconds away from holding her in his arms again.

Kimberleigh's door was opened by her assistant, Luna. "Did you get the ice cream?" she asked, stepping back to admit him.

Despite the curtness of her greeting, he gave her his friendliest smile as he moved past her into the house. "Yes. One pint of The Way the Cookie Crumbles and one S'more Than a Feeling as requested."

Luna wasn't just Kimberleigh's assistant, she was also her best friend and the only other living person they'd trusted with the secret of their relationship. Spencer was a little afraid of her, frankly. Luna hadn't liked him at first and hadn't tried to hide it. She was the most important person in Kimberleigh's life, so he wanted very much to get on her good side and stay there. After a solid month of ingratiating himself, he finally felt like he might be making some headway.

He waited while she closed and locked the door before leaning in and whispering, "How is she?"

Luna's mouth tightened. "Nervous as hell, but trying not to show it."

Kimberleigh was flying to New York tomorrow for a week of production before her first time hosting *SNL*. She hadn't done much live performing—or comedy, for that matter—and was understandably anxious about it.

"Stop whispering about me and bring the ice cream in before it melts," Kimberleigh shouted from the next room.

Luna rolled her eyes and took the grocery bag from Spencer. "What makes you think we were whispering about you?" she shouted back.

He trailed her into the great room, where Kimberleigh was ensconced on the couch under a blanket and a laptop. Her eyes lit up when she saw him, and his chest warmed in response.

"What else would you two have to talk about?" she asked as she untangled herself and got up to greet him.

He paused halfway to the kitchen and waited for her to reach him. "Maybe we've signed up for a pottery class together to deepen our bond of friendship. You don't know."

"Now *that* I would pay money to see." Kimberleigh slipped her arms around his waist and rose up on her toes to kiss him. She smelled sweet and floral, just like her house, and she tasted like heaven on his tongue.

Luna snorted from the kitchen. "There's not enough money in the world."

Kimberleigh broke the kiss and rested her forehead against his. "Hi."

"Hi," he replied quietly, letting his eyes fall closed as a sense of rightness washed over him the way it always did when they were together. He'd never felt anything like this, but he couldn't get enough of it.

"Did they have the S'more Than a Feeling?" she asked.

"It's right here," Luna said.

"Yes, gimme!" Kimberleigh abandoned him in favor of the ice cream he'd brought her.

Spencer followed her into the kitchen, smiling as the two women set upon the ice cream like ravenous predators while he opened the salad he'd picked up for himself. "Please tell me this isn't your dinner."

"Of course not. I've hit my macros every day this week, which means I get a cheat dessert tonight." Kimberleigh's eyes fluttered shut with a sigh as she closed her lips around a spoonful of ice cream.

Goddamn, he wanted to be that spoon right now.

"Hey Spencer, settle a bet for us." Luna's tone sounded suspiciously casual, and it immediately put him on alert for trouble.

He gave her a wary glance as he swallowed a piece of cold, dry chicken breast. "This feels like a trap. Am I being set up?"

"Sheesh, relax," she mumbled around a mouthful of cookie ice cream. "It's not a trap, it's a simple question."

"Laying traps with simple questions is kind of my bread and butter."

Luna rolled her eyes. "Okay, Moriarty. All I want to know is if Spencer is your real name?"

"You don't have to answer that," Kimberleigh interjected, laying her hand on his arm as she shot a warning look at Luna. "Not if you don't want to."

Spencer had a hunch there was more behind Luna's question than simple curiosity. Obviously they'd been talking about him before he arrived, but it felt like there was some additional context he was missing. Like a specific reason Luna wanted to know his real name.

Whatever it was, he didn't care. He had nothing to hide from Kimberleigh, and by extension the person she trusted most in the world.

"I don't mind." He shrugged as he stabbed a piece of romaine. "The answer is yes and no."

Luna's eyes narrowed like she thought he was being evasive. "How can it be both?"

"Because Spencer *is* my real name, but it's not my real *first* name."

"Is it your middle name?" Kimberleigh asked.

"Last name, actually."

"Oh." She frowned slightly as she carved out another spoonful of ice cream. "I just assumed Devlin was your real last name, because your ring has a D on it."

"It was my grandfather's ring. Devlin is my mother's maiden name."

Kimberleigh's gaze met his and softened with understanding. "You took your grandfather's name."

"So what's your real first name?" Luna asked, and once again her tone sounded oddly purposeful.

He regarded her as he chewed the bite of salad in his

mouth, wondering why she was suddenly so interested in knowing his real name. Then it came to him. "You want to do a background check on me," he said, pointing his fork at her.

Luna affected a patently false expression of innocence. "Who, me?"

Spencer lifted his eyebrows slightly and gazed at her, saying nothing. His mild blank stare was one of his most powerful interview tricks. He simply had to look expectant and wait. Eventually most people would get so uncomfortable they'd feel compelled to fill the silence. It was amazing what people would blurt out to smooth over a little social awkwardness.

It only took Luna a few seconds to crack. "Yes, fine!" she admitted, throwing her hands in the air.

"I told her she wasn't allowed." Kimberleigh gave her friend a small, disappointed head shake. "I told her to drop it."

"It's okay." Spencer shrugged. "I don't care."

Luna squinted at him like she didn't believe him. "Really?"

He let his gaze settle on Kimberleigh. "I've got nothing to hide from you." When she smiled, he looked at Luna, who was still peering at him with suspicion. "Or you. Run a background check if it'll make you feel better. I think it's good, actually, that you're so protective. She's lucky to have you watching out for her."

"Hmmm," Luna said, but he thought he detected a glimmer of respect behind her frown.

"As for my name…" Spencer winced as he picked at his salad. "Before I tell you, I feel obligated to explain that it's a family name given to first-born sons for four generations."

"Does that mean it's super embarrassing?" Luna's dark eyes brightened above her freckled cheeks. "It is, isn't it?"

"You really don't have to tell us," Kimberleigh said again.

"Shush," Luna hissed at her before turning back to Spencer. "Please tell us."

His lips quirked in anticipation of their reaction. "It's Virgil."

"Oh. My. God!" Luna had never looked so happy in his presence before. He hadn't even known she could smile that wide.

Kimberleigh didn't say a word. She'd pressed her hand to her mouth and was simply staring at him, wide-eyed. In shock, probably. Or maybe just trying really hard not to laugh.

Spencer didn't mind laughter. He liked making people laugh, even if it was at his own expense. "But wait," he said, arching a dramatic eyebrow. "I haven't told you my middle name yet."

Luna let out a squeak of excitement as she bounced on her toes. "Tell us. Tell us tell us *tell usssss*."

If he'd known humiliating himself was the way to Luna's heart, he'd have done it weeks ago. So he told them his full given name, pausing between each word for maximum effect. "Virgil. Chester. Spencer. The fourth."

"Amazing," Luna wheezed, clutching her stomach as her shoulders shook with laughter. "It's so much better than I ever could have imagined."

"Wow." Kimberleigh bit back a smile and cupped his

jaw as she stepped forward to kiss him. "How did you ever survive to puberty with a name like that?"

"Obviously I went by Spencer in school."

"Obviously," she murmured and kissed him again.

"Now that I've told you my mortifying secret, it's your turn to fess up. Is Kimberleigh your real name? Or did you come up with it on your own?" When he felt her stiffen, he instantly regretted asking the question. "You don't have to tell me, of course, if you don't want."

Kimberleigh shook her head. "No, it's fine." She traded a look with Luna, one of those moments of silent communication they seemed to share frequently in his presence, and he felt a twinge of envy. He'd never had a friend that close —never had *anyone* that close—who understood him the way Luna and Kimberleigh seemed to understand each other.

Luna didn't have much of a poker face, so it wasn't difficult to surmise that she wasn't happy about Kimberleigh sharing this information with him. He could guess why—her past wasn't common knowledge. Her official bio was vague and full of half-truths or outright lies: only child, moved around a lot, started acting at fifteen. No mention of family or even a hometown. In interviews she tended to sidestep the subject, mentioning only that her parents were both now deceased. Whatever was lurking in her background wasn't something she wanted people like him digging into.

Kimberleigh dragged her gaze away from Luna's disapproving frown and looked up at him, a faint smile on her lips. "Luna's actually the one who came up with my stage name, including the spelling of Kimberleigh." She paused, taking a breath before she continued. "My real name is Leah. Leah Krasny."

"That doesn't leave this room," Luna said, her voice a growled warning.

Kimberleigh shot her friend a quelling look. "He knows that."

"Of course," Spencer said, first to Kimberleigh, then again with a solemn look at Luna. "Of course."

"It's not that there's anything shocking or scandalous in my past." Kimberleigh jammed her spoon into her ice cream, creating a pattern of little half-moon gashes. "It's a very run-of-the-mill sort of tragedy. It's just that I really don't want it to become something I'm asked about over and over again in interviews." Her eyes lifted to his. "I'm sure you can understand."

"I can," Spencer said softly.

He'd never tried to bury the details of his own background, but he'd never volunteered them to the public either. His real name was easy enough to find out, and his parents were still kicking around in Valdosta if anyone ever cared enough to look them up. But no one ever had. He wasn't the sort of celebrity people were hungry to know more about. Not like Kimberleigh, with her legions of young fans and box office records. Any story about her was guaranteed to generate clicks—the more tragic and tear-jerking the better.

All Spencer knew of her past was what she'd told him their first night together—that she'd grown up in foster care. But he could make a guess as to the sort of circumstances that had led her there, and it was exactly the sort of juicy story he would have wanted to seize on if he were interviewing her, knowing it'd make for good TV.

Kimberleigh set her ice cream aside and inserted herself

into his arms. He gathered her close and kissed the top of her head.

When he spoke, his voice was a little rough, belying his attempt at humor. "You're checking me for a wire right now, aren't you?"

She laughed against his chest and raised her face to his, sliding a hand around his neck to pull him in for a kiss.

"*Annnnd* that's my cue," Luna said, wrinkling her nose at their PDA. "I'm outta here and I'm taking the cookie ice cream with me."

Kimberleigh slipped out of Spencer's arms as she turned to watch Luna gather her things. "What time is the car coming to take us to the airport tomorrow?"

"Two. I'll be over at ten to help you pack—unless you want me earlier?"

"Nope. Ten's good."

Spencer hooked his arm around Kimberleigh's waist and tugged her up against his side. Tomorrow was Sunday and he didn't have to be anywhere in the morning, which meant they'd be able to sleep in. A rare treat for the two of them.

Luna hoisted her messenger bag over her shoulder and pointed a menacing finger at him. "Don't keep her up late. She needs to get a full night's sleep tonight."

He ceased nuzzling Kimberleigh's hair long enough to give Luna a jocular salute. "Yes, Mom."

"And you—" Luna's finger turned its browbeating power on Kimberleigh. "I want you to take a sleeping pill tonight."

She huffed in defiance. "I really don't need—"

"It's going to be a stressful week of long days and late nights," Luna said over her objection. "I want you to get as much sleep as you can now so you've got some reserves in your tank." The finger of intimidation swiveled toward Spencer again. "Remind her to take a sleeping pill, please."

"I will," he said solemnly, because Luna was right. Kimberleigh needed all the sleep she could get now, and he wasn't going to be the reason she started the upcoming week at a deficit.

"Later, gators." Luna tossed a wave over her shoulder as she headed out. "Thanks for the ice cream, Spencer."

Spencer pressed his nose into Kimberleigh's hair and murmured, "She's warming up to me, right?"

"Of course she is." After they heard the door shut, Kimberleigh turned in his arms. "Come here, you." She gripped his shoulders and climbed him like a damn tree, wrapping her legs around his waist as she kissed him. Her tongue eased into his mouth as her body rocked against his, and he squeezed her perfect ass, feeling like the luckiest man on earth.

"Does that mean you missed me?" he asked when she finally broke the kiss.

She laughed and rubbed her nose against his. "Maybe a little. Or maybe I'm just feeling grateful you brought me ice cream."

Spencer set her on the counter and cradled her face in his hands. "I missed you. And I'm going to miss you even more next week."

"Me too." She turned to grab the ice cream off the counter. "So how was your day? I forgot to ask."

He leaned back, watching as she spooned a bite into her mouth. Noting the faint signs of tension she was trying to hide. She was a very good actress, but he knew her too well now to be taken in. "My day was fine. How are you doing?"

"Great." Her shoulders twitched in a small shrug. Pursing her lips in a sexy moue, she held her spoon up to his mouth. "Here, try some of my ice cream."

It was a transparent attempt at distraction. He let her feed him a bite, swallowing the too-sweet treat before saying, "On a scale of one to ten, how nervous are you for next week?"

Licking the spoon clean, Kimberleigh hopped off the counter and went to put the ice cream away in the freezer. "Let's call it a three."

"Hmm." Spencer intercepted her after she dropped the spoon in the sink and took both her hands in his. "What if we tried that again, but this time you told me the truth?" He brought one of her hands to his lips and kissed her knuckles. "What's the worst that could happen if you just admitted how scared you really are?"

"I hate it when you do that." The quirk of her lips said otherwise, however. As did the way she leaned into him, resting her head against his chest. "I suppose I'm a seven right now. Although I was closer to an eight before you got here."

His heart constricted like she'd reached into his chest and squeezed it.

He loved her. It was ridiculously, blatantly obvious to him and had been for several weeks. But it was way too soon to say anything like that to her. As much as he wanted to share this intense, remarkable feeling, he didn't want to freak her out. Especially not now.

He laid his hand on her hair and kissed the top of her head. "It's okay to be scared. And it's okay to admit it."

Her spine stiffened. "Not to everyone."

"No, not to everyone." His hands stroked down her back. "But to me. And to Luna. It helps to say it out loud."

She made a small noise of disbelief. "Does it?"

"Doesn't it?"

"I guess." Kimberleigh sighed and wound her arms around his waist. "Maybe a little."

"Anyone would be scared in your shoes right now. What you're doing next week is scary and amazing."

"It's fucking terrifying," she mumbled against his chest.

"I know. But fear can be a good thing. It's what keeps us at the top of our game and drives us to excel."

"Yes, but…"

She trailed off without completing the thought, but he knew what she was worried about. In the month they'd been together, he'd gotten to know her inside and out. Not just the self-possessed, captivating beauty the rest of the world saw when they looked at her, but the complicated, clever woman who worked her ass off to maintain the glamorous illusion. It was Kimberleigh's sharp edges and not-so-shiny parts that had called to him and captured his heart, and when he looked at her he saw them as clearly as he saw her exquisite eyes and magnificent smile.

"You're worried about having another panic attack." He was worried about it too, because he wouldn't be there to hold her hand this time.

She was still for a moment. Then he felt her nod against his chest.

Spencer touched the underside of her chin and tilted

her head up to look at him. "You're taking your meds to New York, right? You'll have them with you on set every day?"

"Yes." Her green eyes glimmered as something stirred in the bottomless depths. "But it's not as good as having you with me."

His heart shook as he bent his head and kissed her. The moment felt charged with something beautiful and delicate. He wanted to hold on to it, just like he wanted to hold on to her and shield her from unhappiness and uncertainty. But he couldn't. She was leaving tomorrow and her fears were hers to face on her own.

Plunging his hand in his pocket, he squeezed his fingers around his grandfather's ring. "Here." He unwound one of her hands from his neck and placed the ring in her palm. "You are the strongest, bravest woman I've ever met, and I have one hundred percent confidence that you're going to kick ass and take names next week. But if you ever start to feel overwhelmed, hold on to this and focus like I showed you."

"Spencer," she whispered, blinking as she turned it over in her hand. "I can't take this."

"Sure you can."

Her eyes were shiny when they lifted to his. "It's important to you."

"Not as important as you."

Kimberleigh stared at him for so long, he started to worry he might have fucked up and gone too far. Revealed too much too soon. But then her expression gentled, and she touched her fingertips to his cheek. "You are so—" She pressed her lips together and shook her head.

Spencer lifted his eyebrows and waited for her to finish the thought.

"Nice," she said finally, and he tried not to look disappointed as she leaned up to place a lingering kiss on his cheek. "You're just so genuine and good and sweet. You're a *nice person*, and I don't know what to do with that. I didn't think people like you existed. You're unexpected and improbable and you feel like a miracle."

Well.

That was all right. Better than all right, actually.

Her breath was warm and shallow against his face. When her lips moved to his, he banded an arm around her, pulling her closer. His other hand slid into her hair, tilting her head as she welcomed him into her lush mouth.

She fitted against him like she belonged there. Like she'd been made just for him. Or he'd been made for her. Like they were made for each other.

ten

AFTER A BUSY AFTERNOON of costume fittings, makeup tests, and shooting promos at 30 Rock, Kimberleigh made it back to her hotel at the relatively respectable hour of eight p.m. When she let herself into her suite, she was greeted by an extravagant arrangement of pink roses that had been left on the low table of the sitting area.

Smiling, she dropped her bag on the couch and plucked the card from its little plastic holder as she bent to inhale the fragrant flowers.

Happy Valentine's Day from Your Secret Admirer.

Kimberleigh smiled. Her admirer might be a secret from the hotel and flower shop staff, but he wasn't a secret to her. She snapped a photo of the arrangement with her phone and sent it to Spencer, along with a text: *They're beautiful, thank you! How did you know to get pink?*

It was only five o'clock on the West Coast, which meant Spencer would still be on the *Hot Hollywood Nights* set, not necessarily able to read her text right away. She had time to

99

order herself room service and change into comfier clothes before her phone rang ten minutes later.

"It's not too corny, is it?" he said when she answered. "I wasn't sure how you felt about Valentine's Day."

The sound of his voice made her heart beat faster and easier all at once. It filled her with longing but also peace, loosening some of the tension she'd been carrying around all day.

"It's the exact right amount of corny," she replied, sinking down on the couch in front of the massive arrangement of roses.

"Oh good." It charmed her how relieved he sounded, as if he'd actually been worried she might not appreciate the gesture. "It's Luna you should thank. I asked her to order them so they couldn't be connected to my credit card. Just in case, you know. She said you preferred pink roses over red."

"I told you she liked you."

"I guess you were right. This would have been a perfect opportunity for sabotage."

"I'm sorry we're on opposite coasts for our first Valentine's Day." Only after the words were out of her mouth did Kimberleigh realize the implication. *Our first*—meaning they would be together for other, future Valentine's Days.

It might be presuming too much. But she found, as she turned the idea over in her head, that she hoped not. She liked the feel of a future with Spencer in it.

"We'll just have to make up for it next year," he said, letting her know he felt the same way.

Her heart gave a happy little squeeze that was so unlike her she rubbed her hand on her chest, getting used to the feeling. "I'm not usually a big Valentine's Day person, but…" She trailed off without finishing the thought, letting it hover between them unspoken.

But you make me feel different, she would have said if she'd had the courage. *You're changing me.*

"Me neither," he said softly, as if he understood. For a moment, they were both quiet, still not used to talking about their feelings or acknowledging this thing that had been growing between them. Spencer cleared his throat, and when he spoke again his tone was lighter, trying to return them to less complicated terrain. "How's it going out there?"

"It's okay, actually." So far, anyway. There hadn't been all that much for her to do the first half of the week. All the pressure had been on the writers who'd spent the last four days scrambling to come up with sketches for her, pitching their ideas, then developing and revising the scripts. "We start rehearsals tomorrow. I'm a little nervous about that."

"That's understandable. How's the cast? Everyone being nice to you?"

"Yeah, they've been great so far. Eager to please, mostly." She reached up and squeezed Spencer's ring, which she'd been wearing on a gold chain around her neck. "We'll see how they feel once they're up on that stage with me."

"You're going to do fine. You'll see. You can do this."

"Yeah." She blew out a breath. Either way, it'd be over in two days. By Sunday she'd be back in Spencer's arms again.

But for how long?

This week was only the first and shortest in a long line of separations ahead of them. They'd barely have two weeks together after her return from New York before she'd be leaving again—back to Hungary for a month of reshoots on *Empire of Otherwhere*. After that she'd be in LA for less than a week—hardly even enough time to recover from the jet lag—before she was off to Atlanta for three whole months to do a Jerry Duncan picture she was really, *really* not looking forward to.

She'd been missing Spencer a lot more this week than she'd expected. It wasn't like her. She wasn't this person. She didn't get attached to people. She wasn't clingy. Usually by this point in a relationship she'd be itching for space. Reveling in the freedom afforded by their separation. But she didn't want to be free of Spencer. Not even for a minute, much less a whole week.

If she was feeling the effects of a mere week apart this strongly, how was she going to handle three months apart? Three whole months without Spencer's touch, without the smell of his skin or the taste of his mouth, without his warm, soothing presence in her bed.

"Hey," he said from three time zones away. "Talk to me." He could always read her so well. Somehow even with a continent between them, and without being able to see her face, he could still tell when her thoughts started to run away with her. He always knew when something was wrong and knew exactly what to do to make it better.

So instead of dissembling like her instincts wanted her to, she told him the truth.

"I miss you."

He let out a breath, his soft exhalation magnified and sharpened by the mic on his phone. When he spoke, his voice was quiet and a little rough. "You have no idea how relieved I am to hear you say that."

"You are?"

"I was just sitting here wondering how I'm going to survive two more days without holding you in my arms. This week has been hell without you."

"At least we're both miserable."

"But it's the best kind of misery, looking forward to seeing you again."

A smile curved her lips as she ran the pad of her thumb over his ring. "You've ruined me, you know that?"

"How's that?"

"I used to like being alone. It was easier, not having anyone else around. I didn't have to keep up an act or put on a show. I could be myself with no pretending or lying. Even with Luna—" She stopped, trying to decide how much she really wanted to admit.

Spencer waited, not saying anything or pushing. Giving her the space she needed. It didn't come naturally to her, making these kinds of confessions, but it was getting a little easier every day. Because of him.

"Even with Luna," she finally said, "I'm always trying to be strong so she won't worry. Because I know she already worries so much. When I hired her, I made it her full-time job to worry about me, and I think I feel a little guilty about that."

"I'm pretty sure she'd worry about you whether it was her job or not," Spencer said.

"She would." Kimberleigh smiled, remembering how Luna had mothered her almost from the day they first met, their sophomore year of high school. Kimberleigh had just been placed in a new group home, her last placement before she'd aged out of the system and transitioned to emancipated adulthood. Luna, a bit of an outcast herself, had taken one look at the new transfer student sitting alone in the cafeteria, and made it her mission to befriend her. The two of them had been inseparable ever since. "She's always looked out for me."

"I'm sure you look out for her too."

"I try. But she's never needed me as much as I need her. So I mostly end up trying not to be a burden."

"Kimberleigh." Every time Spencer said her name was always a little different. Always suffused with so many layers of meaning. This time it sounded fond but gently chiding—and also a little sad. "You're not a burden. You're a gift."

She actually believed him. That was the strangest part of all this. When he said her name like that and told her these sweet things that sounded too good to be true, she believed he meant every word. Everything about Spencer was too good to be true. And yet, here he was, continuing to be real.

"My point is," she said once his words had finished wrapping themselves around her heart, "that we're going to be spending a lot more time apart like this. More time than we'll have together probably. And I keep thinking about how much I miss you now, and how much harder it's going to be when I'm in Hungary next month, or in Atlanta the month after that."

"I know," he said with a forlorn-sounding sigh. "I've been thinking about it too."

Her chest squeezed. Despite what she'd said earlier, she didn't like knowing he was miserable. "I think I'm actually a little mad at you, to be honest. I don't need this additional stress in my life."

The sound of his laugh brought a smile to her face. "I'd say I'm sorry, but I'm really not."

"Selfish," she teased, knowing how far it was from the truth.

"Kimberleigh." This time when he said her name it was full of longing, and she could hear the smile dying on his lips as his tone grew serious once more. "It's not going to be easy."

"No, it's not."

"But when have either of us ever settled for easy?"

She huffed out a wry laugh at that. "Never."

"See?" he said. "There you go."

The smile had come back into his voice. If she closed her eyes, she could picture it perfectly.

"We'll be all right," he said, his voice strong and full of confidence. Leaving no room for doubts.

And once again, she believed him.

eleven

"I SAW you on *SNL* last week. You slayed it." Poppy signaled the waitress for another drink before turning back to Kimberleigh. "Straight fire."

They'd finally managed to get together, almost two months after their meeting on the Golden Globes red carpet. Poppy wasn't an easy person to pin down. Her social calendar was booked solid, and she also wasn't great about returning texts. It had taken weeks of back-and-forth before they'd finally agreed on a time and a place.

"Thanks." Kimberleigh was still on her first vodka soda, and she shook her head when the waitress pointed at her drink. "So what's up next for you? You said you were doing a movie with Scotty Deacon?"

"Yep." Poppy bobbed her head, twirling a lock of her long, brown hair around her finger. "I'm off to New York in a couple weeks for a Dior shoot, but after that I head to New Orleans to do this thing with Scotty."

"You said Joe Lincoln was directing, right?" Kimberleigh sipped her vodka soda. "I've heard great things about him."

Poppy shrugged as she drummed a restless fingernail on the tabletop. She'd been a ball of kinetic energy since they sat down, fidgeting and talking a mile a minute. "This whole project is really Scotty's thing. I'm just doing it as a favor to him and Robbie." She flashed a dazzling smile at the waitress as she set a fresh gin and tonic in front of her. "Thanks, babe. You rock."

"So you guys are all still friends?" Kimberleigh asked. "I'd heard Robbie and Scotty had a falling out."

Poppy shook her head as she reached for her drink. "That was just one of those things. It was hard to stay friends with Scotty back then—you remember what he was like. He pulled a lot of shit and fucked a lot of people over. But he and Robbie are as tight as ever now. Scotty and I stayed friends too, but things with me and Robbie are a little weird, you know, after what happened."

Kimberleigh hummed in sympathy. "What did happen? If you don't mind me asking?"

"Oh, well." Poppy waved her hand vaguely. "We just weren't meant to be. Like, I love the guy, but I didn't want to be *married* to him. I feel bad it took me so long to figure it out, but that's how it goes sometimes, right? It's fine though. Robbie and I still see each other a lot because of Scotty. We both stuck by Scotty when he bottomed out—helped him get into rehab and everything. We're like the only two friends he has left these days."

"But he's doing better now, you said."

"Tons better. You wouldn't believe it. After all the stuff he's been through and the things he had to do to climb out of it, he's like a completely different person. Focused, disciplined, sober as a judge. Basically the opposite of me in every possible way." Poppy let out a throaty laugh as she sucked down more gin and tonic. "But obviously no one wanted to work with him after all that bullshit he pulled before, so Robbie found this project for him and signed on as a producer with the stipulation they give the lead to Scotty. I think Robbie basically just handed them a big pile of money to buy the part for Scotty."

"That's nice of him." Kimberleigh wasn't sure she'd be able to give anyone that many second chances.

"Enough about Scotty, I want to hear about you." Poppy leaned forward, resting her elbows on the table. "How are you?"

"I'm good," Kimberleigh said. "It's been nice to have a little time off to recharge, but I'm leaving for Hungary in a few days for *Otherwhere* reshoots. And after that I'll be in Atlanta to do a Jerry Duncan picture."

"Ugh." Poppy's lip curled. "That guy."

"You've worked with him, right?" It was one of the reasons Kimberleigh wanted to catch up with Poppy—to get her perspective on the infamous director. "Is he really that bad?"

Duncan's adrenaline-fueled action blockbusters were as close to a sure thing as you could get in this business, every one of them a runaway box office hit. He worked with the top talent and commanded the biggest budgets. It was why Kimberleigh had signed on to the project, despite Duncan's reputation for being a total nightmare to work with. He'd cemented a lot of stars' careers by putting them through hell on- and off-screen.

"You can pretty much assume every bad thing you've heard about him is true. But don't worry"—Poppy reached across the table and gave Kimberleigh's hand a squeeze —"I'm sure you'll be fine."

Kimberleigh nodded, letting this bad news sink in. "Got any advice for dealing with him?"

"Yeah. Don't be alone in a room with him." Poppy let out a little laugh like she was joking, but the brittleness of her smile very clearly said she wasn't.

"Poppy," Kimberleigh said softly, both an expression of sympathy and an unspoken question.

"It's not like *that*." Poppy waved a hand. "He's a bully, not a predator."

"Is there that much of a difference?"

"Yes," Poppy said, and that one word carried so much meaning, so many awful and sad implications, that Kimberleigh was the one who reached across the table this time to take Poppy's hand. Poppy squeezed back and gave her a tremulous smile. "Jerry's just—he's a dickhead with a bad temper. Too emotional, glass ego, easily stressed. Your typical manbaby on a power trip."

That was a relief. For a second there, Kimberleigh had been considering how bad it would be if she pulled out of the project at this late date. Fragile male egos were manageable—she'd dealt with enough of those in the past. But knowingly putting herself into the path of a sexual predator was another matter altogether.

"Just don't let him talk to you alone if you can help it." Poppy paused to down the rest of her gin and tonic before waving at the waitress again. "He's bad enough about losing his temper in front of people. But without witnesses around, the crazy-mean shit he says is even more out of control. And don't ever let him know he's getting to you. If he senses any insecurity or weakness, he'll try to exploit it. Do what he says, but try not to react to him at all. Don't show any emotion unless it's for a scene."

"Be an ice queen," Kimberleigh said wryly. "I should be able to handle that."

"I know you can," Poppy said. "That's why I know you'll be fine."

"Same again?" the waitress asked as she reached for Poppy's empty glass.

"Yes, please." Poppy plucked the straw out of her empty glass and flashed another of those dazzling smiles. "Thank you."

Kimberleigh shook her head when the waitress looked at her. "I'm good, thanks."

"You're making me look like a lush," Poppy said.

"I'm in training for my next project."

"Sure, me too." Poppy's gaze followed the retreating waitress for a moment before she turned back to Kimberleigh, resting her chin in her hand as she tapped the straw on the rim of her water glass. "So what else is up with you?"

"Not much." Kimberleigh shrugged as she stirred the melting ice in her drink.

"I heard about your breakup with Aidan. What an incredible asshole. Are you okay?"

"Yeah, it's fine." Kimberleigh's shoulders lifted again. "It's whatever. I wasn't all that attached to him, as it turned out."

She could have admitted to Poppy that the relationship had been fake, but it was safer to keep it all locked down, even with people she felt she could trust. You never knew who might be eavesdropping, or who might carelessly let something slip to the wrong person, or who might not be as trustworthy as they seemed. Kimberleigh had been slowly learning to loosen up around Spencer, but she was still a long way from being as open and chatty as Poppy.

"You guys seemed pretty serious. You were together for what—a year?"

"Something like that."

Exactly that, in fact, according to the terms of their contract. Even the manner of their breakup had been carefully orchestrated to maximize publicity. A mild scandal in the form of his apparent infidelity, which generated sympathy for Kimberleigh that warmed her ice queen image and cast her ex in the role of desirable bad boy, boosting both his brand and that of his new contracted girlfriend. Kimberleigh wished them both luck, though she didn't miss either him or the charade. He'd been professional throughout their "relationship," but conversationally about as interesting as watching paint dry.

At some point she should probably take on a new "boyfriend." It would help provide a smokescreen for her relationship with Spencer. Which reminded her of the other thing she'd been wanting to talk to Poppy about.

Kimberleigh leaned forward and rested her forearms on the table. "Can I ask you something?"

Poppy nodded as she chewed on her straw. "Shoot."

"The interview you did with Spencer Devlin last year—"

At the mention of his name, Poppy's expression went flat. "What about it?"

"Did you know he was going to ask you those questions about your father?"

"Did it look like I knew?"

"No."

"I had no idea. It took me completely off guard."

The waitress reappeared, and Poppy's expression changed from sullen to radiant in the blink of an eye. "You're an angel," she said with a warm smile, and the waitress's cheeks flushed pink.

It was a reminder of what a good actress Poppy was. She gave an impression of easy openness that made her a lot of friends, but was she really as candid as she seemed? Or was she just playing a role to protect herself the way Kimberleigh did? If anyone had good reason to build a defensive wall around herself, it was Poppy, who'd been pushed into this business at an early age by a controlling stage father who'd tossed her to the sharks for his own financial gain.

"Is it possible your publicity team approved the questions without your knowledge?"

"Fuck no," Poppy said as she sipped her fresh gin and tonic.

"The publicity didn't hurt you though, did it?"

"I guess." Poppy's eyes narrowed as she set down her drink. "What's this about?"

Kimberleigh schooled her expression as she offered the lie she'd prepared. "Spencer Devlin's been trying to get me to come back on his show, but I'm on the fence about it. I really don't like the guy, but my publicist wants me to do it." She gave a light shrug. "When I brought up his interview with you as one of the reasons I think he's shady, he claimed the questions had come from your team."

"He's lying," Poppy said.

Someone was lying, anyway.

But was it Poppy, Poppy's publicist, or Spencer?

Kimberleigh desperately wanted to believe Spencer had told her the truth. She *should* believe him, shouldn't she? Didn't she know him well enough by now to trust him?

It was too awful to imagine that he might have lied to her. She had to trust him, because the alternative was unthinkable—that the man she'd invited into her life and let down her walls for might not be the man she'd let herself believe he was.

twelve

SPENCER FUCKING HATED NOT BEING able to pick Kimberleigh up at the airport when she came back from Hungary. Being stuck waiting for her at her house after their monthlong separation was the first time this whole secrecy thing had really bothered him. Usually it was fine by him. He might even concede it was better this way. More convenient. Easier not having to suffer the intrusive questions and odd looks he knew he'd get from his colleagues if they knew the truth.

But the fact that Luna was the one at the airport right now fetching Kimberleigh's luggage off the carousel, guiding her past the paparazzi who always stalked LAX, and shepherding her into a hired car driven by a stranger made Spencer downright murderous.

With a groan of frustration, he leaned his head back on Kimberleigh's couch and rubbed his tired eyes. Luna had given him a key so he could be here waiting for Kimberleigh when she got home. He'd worked his ass off the last few days in order to take the afternoon and evening off so he could devote every second of the next fourteen hours to showing Kimberleigh exactly how much he'd missed her.

As soon as she got here, anyway.

Her flight had landed an hour ago. He'd been following its slow progress across the country in the airline app, but he'd also gotten a text confirmation from Kimberleigh as soon as she touched down.

I'm here!!!! I'll be home soon!

Five whole exclamation points. He thumbed back to her text, his chest warming all over again at the sight of all that punctuation. He'd learned from their extensive text conversations over the last month that she wasn't ordinarily an extravagant user of exclamation points. They must mean she was as excited as he was.

Unfortunately for both of them, she'd landed on the leading edge of rush hour, and the drive up to Brentwood was taking forever. Impatiently, Spencer checked the traffic again, but the 405 was as much of a parking lot as ever, still a solid red line from Howard Hughes Parkway to Wilshire. God only knew how much longer it'd take for her to crawl her way to him at this time of day.

He'd brought his laptop to distract him while he waited, but his impatience to see Kimberleigh again had rendered his brain incapable of thinking about anything else. This last month had been the longest of his life with her half a world away from him. Between their work schedules and the time difference, it had been difficult to squeeze in video calls more than once or twice a week. His mornings had been her afternoons, and his bedtime had been her early morning, so they'd mostly resorted to communicating through texts, often with hours passing between replies.

Every morning Spencer had woken up thinking about her. Missing her. His dick hard and aching along with his heart. He'd never missed anything in his life as much as he'd missed Kimberleigh these last few weeks.

He wasn't accustomed to feeling this way. Missing someone. Everyone Spencer had ever left behind had been someone he'd been glad to get away from. This was the first time he'd ever been the person left behind, even if it was only temporary.

Still, he felt like it had been good for them, this test. Proof that they could make separations like this work, which they'd need to do if they were going to have a future together. It had given them both a preview of what it would be like from now on with Kimberleigh away for months at a time, and him unable to go visit her. If they could survive this, they could survive the next separation, even if it was three times as long.

In a way, Spencer felt they'd grown closer during their time apart. Even if Kimberleigh couldn't reply immediately, she always replied to his texts, usually with lengthy stories of her days on set, the people she was working with, or the things she'd seen in that faraway country he'd never been to but that she'd grown to love while filming three movies there back-to-back. He'd fallen a little bit in love with it himself, just hearing her talk about it.

The video calls they'd managed to have had acted like a cortisone shot to his aching soul. The sound of her voice, the sight of her smile—not to mention the times when those calls had gotten hot and intimate—had sustained him for days afterward.

The sound of a car door outside captured Spencer's

attention. Another door slammed, and he heard the soft murmur of female voices.

In his haste to thrust his laptop onto the coffee table, he managed to drop his phone on the floor. By the time he'd sorted himself out, a key was already turning in the lock. He arrived in the front entry just as the door flew open.

Kimberleigh's eyes homed in on him, and she broke into a heart-stopping smile. He'd halted when the door opened, and for a second they just stared at each other like they couldn't quite believe they were in the same place again.

Then they both started moving at once, straight into each other's arms.

He wrapped her up as tight as he could without hurting her, lifting her up off the floor a little before burying his face against her neck. She smelled like an airplane and the inside of a hired car, but underneath all that she smelled comforting and so familiar his chest gave a twinge. Even though she was the one who'd been away, she smelled exactly like coming home.

"I missed you," she said, kissing his chest, his neck, and finally his mouth. And *fuck*, she tasted even better than she smelled. Almost as good as she felt.

"I missed you so much," he murmured in between kisses. "I'm so happy you're here. Fuck, I'm just so—"

"Dudes," Luna said, dragging one of Kimberleigh's gigantic roller bags over the threshold. "Don't make me turn the hose on you."

Reluctantly, Spencer let go of Kimberleigh in order to help Luna with the luggage. He left the two women chattering in the kitchen while he carried Kimberleigh's bags upstairs, reminding himself they'd missed each other's company too.

As he was coming back down, he heard the front door close, and when he found Kimberleigh she was alone. "Did Luna leave already?"

Kimberleigh nodded as she came toward him. "She thought we might like some alone time."

"She didn't have to rush off. If you two want to catch up first—"

"We had the whole car ride to catch up." Kimberleigh's hands smoothed up Spencer's arms to the tops of his shoulders. "Now it's your turn."

She jumped into his arms, knowing he'd catch her the way he always did, his hands cradling her ass as her legs wrapped around his waist. Her hands slid into his hair as she pulled his mouth to hers. Unlike their previous, frantic, hurried kisses by the door, this one was hot and slow and sweet.

Spencer almost said it right then, right in the middle of that kiss.

The thing he'd been thinking every day since she left.

I love you.

He'd been carrying it around in his chest for more than a month, getting used to the shape of it. Every day it had felt more true. More *real.* And now that Kimberleigh was back and in his arms, it felt truer than anything else ever had.

But he knew her too well to spring something like that on her. Convincing her to let him inside her defenses had been a slow, painstaking process. Bit by bit, he'd eked his way into her life—and into her heart, he hoped. But he still sensed her hesitation occasionally. Felt her reluctance to give too much of herself away. He was winning her over, he had no doubt of that, but if he got overeager and tried to leap too far ahead too fast, it might trip them up.

No, he wouldn't tell her yet. For the time being he'd keep this just for himself. Maybe he'd tell her before she left for Atlanta. Then again, maybe he wouldn't. They only had a short time together. Less than a week. And he planned to make the most of it. He didn't want anything casting a shadow over these few precious days.

It didn't really matter, either way. He knew how he felt, and that was enough. He didn't need to say it or hear her say it back.

Not when she was holding on to him like this, her hands on his skin, her mouth soft and searching against his. She was his. That was all that mattered.

And he was irrevocably hers.

thirteen

THE THREE-HOUR TIME difference between Los Angeles and Atlanta wasn't nothing, but it was a hell of a lot better than Hungary had been. It meant when Spencer was waking up at dawn to squeeze in an hour and a half at the gym on his way to work, Kimberleigh was already awake. He got to talk to her almost every morning, either while he was making coffee and getting dressed, or on his commute to or from the gym.

It made all the difference, starting his days like that. Hearing her voice, seeing her face, telling her how much he missed her, and hearing that she missed him too.

He began counting on those daily check-ins to keep him balanced. Calm. Soothed.

He hadn't realized quite how much he'd come to depend on them until their nice little routine was disrupted.

Kimberleigh was on night shoots this week, so when Spencer was getting up, she'd just gone to bed. On the bright side, it meant they got to talk at night, before he went to bed and she went to set, which was an hour more

120

conducive to the phone sex they were really getting quite spectacular at.

But he couldn't help feeling a bit lost in the mornings without the sound of Kimberleigh's laugh to jump-start his day. Today he'd walked out of the house with mismatched socks and spilled his post-workout protein shake in the car.

It was fine though. Other than a few minor mishaps, they were totally handling the long-distance thing. Making it work for them.

Although...he'd started to worry about her a little on this shoot. For one thing, she seemed tired all the time, which she'd blamed on long shooting days and her usual insomnia. But it was more than just that. She seemed stressed and unhappy in a way she hadn't in Hungary. She tried to hide it, of course, but Spencer had become an expert in decoding the many moods of Kimberleigh Cress.

There were no stories about her coworkers on this shoot or the places she'd visited in Atlanta. She'd had very little to say at all, other than the fact that the days were long and the action sequences grueling.

"How are you getting on with your costars?" he asked her that night, propped up in bed with his laptop balanced on a pillow.

"Fine," she'd said in a disinterested tone that hadn't sounded all that fine. She was in the kitchen of her Atlanta condo, eating one of the prepared meals the studio-assigned dietician had arranged for her.

"Richard Scardino isn't making your life difficult, is he? He can be a real prima donna." Spencer's impression from every interaction he'd ever had with the Oscar-winning actor was that he was a self-important piece of shit who thought being an asshole made him deep.

"He's okay. I'm used to dealing with actors like him."

Spencer tried again. "What do you think of Griffin Beach? I've heard he's a good guy."

Kimberleigh shrugged, her eyes on something off to the side of her laptop screen. Her phone, maybe. "I haven't gotten to know him, really. We don't interact much off-camera."

"Maybe you should try to befriend him. He might make a good ally."

"Why do you think I need an ally?" She reached for her coffee, still not looking at him.

"A friend, then. If the days are long and the work is hard, the time might pass more pleasantly if you were on friendly terms with your costar."

"Spencer." She looked right into the camera. "You know I don't do friendly."

That wasn't entirely true though. She was friendly with the *Otherwhere* cast and crew. She was friendly with Poppy Carpenter. With Luna. With him, even if it had taken a panic attack for her to give him a chance.

"How's Jerry Duncan been treating you?" Spencer asked, just like he asked her almost every day.

Everyone knew about Duncan's reputation. Kimberleigh was tough as hell, and Spencer didn't doubt that she could take care of herself, but that didn't mean he liked the idea of her working with a director famous for flying off the handle.

She stepped out of frame to carry her dishes to the sink. "I told you, he's been fine."

"Really?"

"Yes." She sounded even farther away now.

"Kimberleigh."

"What?"

"Come here where I can see you."

She reappeared on-screen, too close, the camera focused on her forehead. Then she adjusted it, backing it up so he could see her whole face and the top part of her chest. "Better?" She still seemed distracted. Restless. Not really paying attention to him.

"Hey." He reached out and tapped his finger on the screen. "Look at me."

Her eyes focused on the screen and stayed there. Not looking directly at the camera this time, but a little below. At him. He saw her go still, her restless energy quieting as she gazed at him. "I'm here."

"You can tell me if things aren't okay there. You don't have to be strong so I won't worry about you."

"I'm okay, I promise." She was very convincing. He almost believed her. "It's not the funnest job I've ever had, but it's not the worst either." Her hand squeezed the ring he'd given her, which hung from a chain around her neck.

He wasn't sure if it was a good thing or a bad thing, the way she was clenching that ring. He'd never been more glad he'd given it to her, but he hoped she didn't need it very much.

"I'm getting through it," she said. "Counting down the days until I see you again."

"Sixty-three days," he replied automatically. He counted them every night before bed.

"Sixty-three days," she repeated, her lips curving in a faint smile.

"I've been thinking…I could come out there for a visit if you want. In secret. No one would have to know."

"You can't take the time off."

"I can make it work."

"*I* can't take the time off. We'd barely see each other. I know it's not easy for you to get away, and it'd be a wasted trip." Her smile grew a little wider. "It's a sweet offer though."

"It's a standing one. Just say the word if you change your mind or find yourself with some free time coming up. I'll move heaven and earth if I have to."

She kissed her fingers and pressed them to the screen. "I know you will."

"You're really okay?"

"I really am. But I also really have to go."

Spencer nodded, trying not to let his disappointment show too much. "Have a good night. I miss you."

"I miss you too. Sleep well. Dream of me."

"I never dream of anything else."

He did dream of her afterward, but it wasn't a pleasant dream. In his dream, Spencer flew out to Atlanta to see her, just like he'd offered, but everything went wrong. His flight was delayed, he got lost trying to find the studio, then he wound up wandering around looking for the right soundstage. When he finally found it, he couldn't find Kimberleigh inside. He looked and looked, but she was nowhere.

He woke up feeling anxious in a way he hadn't felt in years. His fingers itched to hold his grandfather's ring, but it was in Atlanta with Kimberleigh. Just like his heart.

The dream left him in a surly fog that persisted through his workout and his drive into work. He mumbled a greeting at Vanessa as he slunk into his office and sank down behind his desk. While he sipped the coffee he'd bought on his way in, he launched the HHN website to see what was happening in the world of entertainment news.

The first thing he saw was Kimberleigh's face staring at him from the top-stories banner. Spencer's blood froze in his veins as he read the headline beneath the red carpet photo they'd cropped to just her face and shoulders: *Kimberleigh Cress' Secret Childhood Tragedy Revealed!*

Fuck.

What exactly did they have? And how did they get it?

His hand shook as he clicked on the link to the full story. Panic clawed at his insides as he scanned it. They didn't just have Kimberleigh's background in foster care. They'd published her real name. And they'd found even more than that. More than Spencer had known, even. They'd unearthed her mother's name and the tragic story of how Kimberleigh—née Leah Krasny—had ended up in foster care. An absentee father never in the picture. An addict mother who'd overdosed, leaving her eight-year-old daughter in the care of the state.

It was exactly as she'd described it—a tragedy too depressingly commonplace to qualify as a scandal. And yet still just interesting enough, just sordid enough, that it would follow her everywhere now that it was out. It would always be a part of her story, something she'd be asked about over and over again, long past the point that there was anything left to say.

Fuck fuck fuck fuck. *Fuck.*

fourteen

KIMBERLEIGH WINCED when her phone started buzzing again. Texts and calls had been pouring in more or less nonstop for the last few hours—ever since the story about her had hit the internet. Most of her callers were well-meaning, but she wasn't ready to talk to anyone yet— other than her publicist, Tamara, who was already on the case back in LA, working up a strategy to deal with the fallout.

Not that the story was bad for Kimberleigh from a publicity angle. In fact, Tamara had been almost gleeful— though she'd tried hard not to show it. A sad and tragic childhood only made Kimberleigh more sympathetic.

But it wasn't the sort of sympathy Kimberleigh wanted, and it definitely wasn't a subject she wanted to talk about publicly. She'd impressed as much on Tamara, who'd promised to do what she could to contain it. Though they both knew there was only so much anyone could do now that the story was out of the bag.

"Who is it?" Luna asked, yawning at Kimberleigh through the screen of her laptop.

Kimberleigh had woken her at an ungodly hour on the West Coast, which she felt bad about, but she'd needed someone to talk her down after Tamara had woken her to tell her about the story. She'd needed to talk to the only person who understood exactly what this meant to her.

Kimberleigh peeked at her phone screen, just in case it was Tamara calling. The painful lump in her throat grew larger as she dismissed the call. "It's just Spencer again."

Luna gave her a long, careful look. "Maybe you should talk to him."

"Why?" she snapped, more sharply than she intended, and instantly regretted taking her anger out on her friend.

"To let him explain," Luna replied, unfazed.

When Kimberleigh had first seen the story this morning, after a long night on set and only a couple of hours' sleep, she'd gone numb with shock. As the reality had sunk in, so too had the sick, dawning realization of how this must have happened—and *who* was responsible. She'd felt so nauseous, she'd actually run to the bathroom to throw up.

Spencer. The man she'd talked to just last night. Had betrayed her. He'd sold her out for an exclusive. How many times had he sworn she could trust him? And the whole time he'd been gathering information. Doing research on her. Digging around for his big scoop. While sleeping in her bed.

Only that wasn't the part that hurt the most. If all they'd been doing was sleeping together, Kimberleigh would have been safe. She never would have let Spencer get the better of her. The part that really hurt was that he hadn't just wormed his way into her bed. He'd wormed his way into her heart.

"There's nothing to explain," Kimberleigh said coldly. "I'm not interested in hearing his apology." She'd have to talk to him eventually, of course, to make an official end of things between them. But she didn't need to do it on his terms. He could stew for a while until she was good and goddamn ready to talk.

Luna shook her head. "You don't know he's the one—"

"Of course he is. I told him my real name. You were there—you even tried to stop me, because you knew all along he couldn't be trusted."

"I admit I had reservations about him at first, but I really can't believe he'd do this. Not intentionally."

"That just shows what a good liar he is. He even had you fooled." There was some consolation in that, she supposed. She hadn't been the only one who'd fallen for Spencer's charms.

"Did he though?" Luna's forehead furrowed as she chewed on her lower lip. "Just for this one story? It doesn't make sense."

"You can't honestly think it's a coincidence. He's the first person in years that I've told about my past or confided my real name to, and now suddenly here's this story—broken by the very same entertainment news organization he happens to work for."

"I admit, it's weird."

"It's more than just weird. It's brazenly deceitful."

"But his name's not even on the story."

"He doesn't write for the website anymore. He probably gave it to one of the staff writers in exchange for...something. A raise, a better parking space, whatever. I'm sure he was rewarded richly for it."

"It's possible he didn't do it on purpose. Maybe he accidentally let it slip."

"Oh, so he was just *careless* with the extremely sensitive personal information I shared with him in confidence? He *accidentally* let it slip to one of his colleagues who trades in celebrity gossip for a living? Excuse me if I don't rush to forgive him for that. And why are you defending him anyway? You didn't even like him!"

"But *you* did," Luna said. "You liked him a lot. I guess I just really don't want it to be true."

Kimberleigh hadn't just liked him—she'd started to let herself fall in love with him. She'd let him make her feel safe, which was the cruelest betrayal of all.

She remembered now why you weren't supposed to let your guard down. Because you were never safe. No matter how nice someone seemed and no matter how sweet their words sounded, the only person you could really trust was yourself.

Her phone started buzzing next to her. It was Spencer again, his face on her screen, his betrayal slashed across her heart. Would he ever give up and just leave her alone? Hadn't he done enough? What did he expect to get out of talking? What more could he possibly take from her?

"He's going to keep calling," Luna said. "Until you answer it."

Kimberleigh knew she was right. If she wanted to be free of him, she needed to get this over with. She needed to make a clean break so he'd stop hounding her. "Fine. I'm going to let you go so I can talk to him."

"Good luck," Luna said. "Call me when you're done."

Kimberleigh ended the call and picked up her phone. Before she could second-guess herself, she swiped to answer Spencer's call.

"Kimberleigh," he said, sounding frantic. "Oh thank god, I've been trying to call you all morning. There's a story on our website. Sweetheart, I'm so sorry but—"

"I've seen it," she said, cutting him off.

"Are you okay?"

"I'll survive." That was what she did. It was what she'd always been best at.

"I don't know how they got it, but I'll find out. I've got a call in to the managing editor. I know I can't undo it now that it's out there, but I'll tell her—"

"*Stop*. Just stop it." In the silence that followed her outburst, Kimberleigh closed her eyes and tried to calm her pounding heart. When she spoke again her voice was steadier. "Stop pretending this wasn't your doing. You don't actually think I'm that stupid, do you?"

"Kimberleigh." There were too many cadences in the way he said her name to parse all of them individually, but the one that came through strongest of all was *hurt*.

And honestly? That pissed her off even more. How dare he try to act hurt when she was the one who'd been deceived and sold out.

"You can't think—" He stopped and sucked in an unsteady breath before trying again. "You can't think I'd do that to you."

Wow. He should have stuck with acting, because he had a natural gift for it. He was really selling it with that little tremor in his voice and everything. But it wouldn't work.

She was done falling for his pretty lies and feigned sincerity. There was no softness left in her. Only ice.

Her voice dripped with it when she replied. "What else could I possibly think under the circumstances?"

"I didn't do this. I swear to you. I haven't breathed a word to anyone."

"Sure." Her tone was harsh and mocking, and she could almost hear his flinch over the phone.

"Don't do that," he said, his words sharper now. He'd graduated from a play for sympathy to pretend indignation.

"What?" she shot back, fueled by her own indignation. "Call you on your bullshit? Obviously it's something I should have done a long time ago. You must think you're pretty clever, playing me for a fool all this time. Well done. You really pulled one over on me."

She couldn't even claim not to have had any hint that something was amiss. As soon as she found out he'd lied about Poppy, she should have known. She should have gone into high alert. But instead she'd ignored the warning sign. Because she hadn't wanted to believe it of him.

"God, Kimberleigh, no. I would never do that to you. You have to believe me."

"I really don't." She could feel the frost building up inside her, hardening all the soft places she'd allowed him to see, and she welcomed its numbing cold.

"Please." There was that tremor again, but she closed her eyes against it. "Please listen to me."

"I'm done listening to you, Spencer. In fact, we're done talking. There's nothing left to say."

"Please don't do this. I love you."

This time she was the one who flinched. But it didn't

matter, because the frost was still spreading, and it'd cover this hurt over too, freezing it solid, making her tougher. Because that was what you did with hurt. You learned from it and used it to make yourself better. She'd rebuild all the walls Spencer had breached, but this time they'd be even stronger. Impenetrable.

"Don't try to contact me again." She hung up before he could say anything else.

IN A MOVIE, THIS WOULD BE THE PART WHERE KIMBERLEIGH was supposed to cry her eyes out over Spencer. But her life wasn't a movie and that wasn't how she rolled.

Instead, she did what she'd always done. She threw herself into work. Which wasn't hard, because this shoot had already been grueling and demanding before her personal life had blown up in her face. Jerry Duncan was everything Poppy had said he was, but her advice had been spot-on. Kimberleigh's new ice armor served her well. He couldn't hurt her if she refused to let him get to her.

She moved through the remaining days on set like a robot. Focused, single-minded, unfeeling. But as long as the days were on this shoot, they weren't long enough. Eventually she had to go home to that unfamiliar condo and lie in the dark in that uncomfortable bed, trying not to let the memories flicker through her brain like a roll of celluloid film.

When she let herself think back over their last conversation, and she remembered the pain and desperation in Spencer's voice, she couldn't help wondering if he'd been telling the truth. The timing was too big a coincidence to ignore, but as far as evidence went, it was only circumstantial. She didn't actually *know* that Spencer had betrayed her.

That was the problem though. She didn't know anything anymore. She didn't know if she could trust him. She no longer believed he'd meant any of the things he'd said to her. Especially that last, desperate *I love you*.

But she *really* couldn't let herself think about that, because whenever she did, her heart would start pounding and her throat would close up and it felt like she couldn't breathe.

So she didn't think about it.

Or she tried not to, anyway.

They could never go back to the way things were. Never get back what they'd lost.

Even though the thought of never seeing Spencer again made her throat burn and her lungs ache. And sometimes she woke with tears in her eyes, unable to breathe because she missed him so much. She couldn't let herself be that person she'd become with him. Someone willing to take foolish chances and risk everything she'd worked so hard for.

She couldn't even trust herself anymore. When it came to Spencer, she'd gotten everything wrong. One way or another, she'd screwed up big time. Either he'd been a duplicitous liar and her trust in him had been misguided— or he'd been telling the truth and she'd done him a grievous wrong by not believing him.

It'd be better, frankly, if he'd been lying. That was much easier to accept than the thought that she might have been the one who'd betrayed his trust, and how badly she'd hurt him if he'd been telling the truth.

But she couldn't know which it was. She'd probably never know.

The only thing she did know was that she couldn't trust her own instincts. He'd destroyed her confidence in her own judgment. Intentionally or not, she hated him for it.

Kimberleigh considered herself lucky to be in the middle of a shoot when the story broke. It kept her busy and out of LA, and gave her an excuse to stay quiet and out of sight. She hadn't gotten friendly with anyone on her project, which was just as well. It meant they all left her the hell alone, which was what she wanted most right now.

But when Poppy Carpenter texted two weeks after the story broke and asked Kimberleigh to call her, she actually did. Kimberleigh figured she owed Poppy, both for warning her about Spencer and for giving her good advice about Jerry Duncan.

It took a few tries to actually get a hold of her, and when Kimberleigh finally got her on the phone, Poppy didn't sound like her usual effervescent self.

"Is everything okay?" Kimberleigh asked once they'd dispensed with the pleasantries.

"Yeah, sure, great," Poppy said brusquely. "But there's something I need to tell you."

That didn't sound good. Kimberleigh steeled herself for bad news. "Okay."

"That story about you—about how you grew up in foster care because of what happened to your mom? I'm pretty sure it was my fault."

fifteen

"WHAT?" Kimberleigh's voice came out half choked. Whatever she'd been expecting it wasn't this.

"The night you hosted *SNL*, I had a bunch of people over at my place." Poppy spoke quickly, the words spilling out of her like she was trying to get this over with. "We'd been drinking and whatever, and someone turned on the show, and I was telling everyone how we'd worked together when you first started out. And I'd probably had a little too much to drink, because I may have told them some stuff I shouldn't have—like your real name and the fact that you'd been a foster kid."

Kimberleigh's throat hurt. "You *may* have told them? Or you told them?"

"I told them."

"I see."

"I wasn't really thinking about it," Poppy said, sounding miserable. "You told me all that stuff ages ago, and I thought it was a cool story. And it wasn't like I went to the tabloids myself—I only told a few friends who were hanging at my place. But I guess one of the people who was there had brought along some dude she'd just met, and she didn't realize he worked for HHN."

Kimberleigh didn't know how to respond. Her mind and body had both gone completely numb. "Right."

"I'm really sorry. I shouldn't have been running my mouth off like that."

"No, you really shouldn't have."

"You're pissed. I don't blame you for hating me."

Kimberleigh took a deep breath and let it out slowly. "I don't hate you."

It felt like the right thing to say. Also, it was true. She didn't hate Poppy.

There was something so *wrong* about that when you compared it to the way she'd reacted when she thought Spencer was the one who'd betrayed her. Spencer, who'd only ever tried to take care of her and make her laugh. Who, it turned out, had been every bit as trustworthy as he'd seemed. Who'd never lied to her.

Who'd *loved* her.

He'd done nothing wrong, and she'd ejected him from her life without a second thought. Never once had she even considered giving him the benefit of the doubt, much less another chance. She'd jumped straight to hating him when he hadn't done anything at all to deserve it.

But Poppy, who *had* done something wrong, who'd betrayed Kimberleigh's confidence—even if it was a youthful confidence given years ago—she was willing to forgive.

How completely fucking unfair was that?

Kimberleigh had dismissed Spencer's denials and

refused to listen to him because she'd *wanted* to believe the worst of him. All along, she'd been waiting for proof that the relationship was a mistake. That all her old fears had been right, and she shouldn't let herself trust anyone because they always, *always* ended up hurting her.

But she was the one who'd done the hurting. Gentle, caring, sweet Spencer. She'd turned on him. Callously flung accusations at him. *Left* him. Exactly the way everyone had always left her.

God, she was so fucking broken. She didn't deserve him. Her scarred heart wasn't capable of loving him the way he deserved to be loved.

Kimberleigh barely remembered the rest of the conversation with Poppy. As soon as she got off the phone, she sank to the floor of her trailer and hugged her knees.

The weight of just how cruelly she'd treated Spencer sat on her chest like a concrete block. She squeezed her eyes shut against the memory of how anguished he'd sounded. The way his voice had shaken as he'd begged her to believe him.

Every shallow, aching breath she sucked into her lungs was an agony, but it was only what she deserved. She didn't even try to stave off this spiral. She let it have her, succumbing to all the ugly, punishing thoughts crawling over her, choking her, crushing her.

Until a knock on the door of her trailer punctured the rising tide of panic, and a PA called out that they were ready for her on set.

She couldn't afford to indulge her guilty feelings right now. She had a job to do. A responsibility to the people she worked with. So she fought her way out of the miasma. Concentrated on slowing her breathing.

Inhale. Exhale. Just like Spencer had showed her. Kimberleigh let herself picture his face, calm and handsome and reassuring. Imagined him sitting next her, holding her hand against his chest. Remembered the slow, steady beat of his heart, and timed her breathing to match it.

Gradually, the nausea subsided and the tightness in her chest loosened. As her breathing returned to normal, she looked down and realized she'd been clutching Spencer's ring. Clinging to it like a life raft. An unconscious habit she'd developed during their time apart.

Her throat tried to clog again, but with tears instead of panic. But she didn't have time for that either. Kimberleigh shoved the tears back down with everything else she couldn't indulge in right now. She got to her feet, feeling shaky and exhausted like she'd just finished a hard workout. But she was used to working through exhaustion.

So that was what she did.

"I told you," Luna said when Kimberleigh called to tell her about Poppy's confession.

Kimberleigh accepted this as nothing less than what she deserved. "You did. I should have listened."

"I *knew* it. The way he looked at you when you weren't watching—that wasn't fake. He really did love you."

Tears of shame burned in Kimberleigh's eyes, and she leaned out of frame, reaching for her water so Luna wouldn't see her wipe them away.

When she looked at the screen again, Luna was shaking her head. "God. Poor Spencer."

Poor Spencer, indeed.

"I really fucked everything up," Kimberleigh said.

"What are you going to do?"

She'd been giving that particular question a lot of thought and had come to the conclusion that she had no fucking idea. "What do you think I should do?"

"I dunno. Call him?"

"What's the point? You think he's going to take me back after what I did? He shouldn't. He's definitely better off without me." Wouldn't it be kinder to leave him alone and let him get over her in peace than to force herself on him and dredge up all that pain again?

Luna glared at her through the screen. "Okay, first of all, shut up. I regret to inform you that you're totally fucking lovable, so don't even start with that shit. Yes, you screwed up, and he's got good reason to be upset with you right now. But at the very least he deserves to hear you admit you fucked up, doesn't he?"

Kimberleigh ignored the first part, because she didn't agree, although she appreciated Luna for saying it. But the second part, about what she owed Spencer, that wasn't something she could ignore. He deserved an apology. He didn't need to accept it or forgive her, but she needed to offer it anyway.

"Second of all," Luna continued, "you don't get to decide what's best for him. That's his choice to make, not yours."

Was it? If she cared about him, didn't she have an obligation to protect him? The same way he'd always tried to protect her. She wouldn't let him walk into traffic or mix bleach and ammonia without trying to stop him. Why would she let him give her another chance to hurt him?

Assuming he wanted to. Probably he was smarter than that.

"I'll call him," Kimberleigh said. "To apologize, at least."

"Good girl." Luna leaned forward a little, her face growing bigger as she gazed through the screen. "It's easy to make mistakes. It's a lot harder to fix them."

"Yeah." Kimberleigh looked down at the lump under her shirt where Spencer's ring hung around her neck. "I'm pretty sure there's no fixing this."

"Maybe. But you've still got some groveling to do."

Kimberleigh accepted this with a nod, still looking down at that shape close to her heart. "I'll call him."

She needed to get his ring back to him, but she'd been reluctant to ship something that precious and irreplaceable. Also, if she were being honest, she hadn't wanted to give it up. Even when she'd hated him, when she'd been convinced he'd betrayed her, she'd still carried his ring with her every day. So maybe she hadn't really hated him after all.

"Can I ask you something?" Luna said, and Kimberleigh looked up at the screen. "Do you love him?"

Kimberleigh swallowed, her hand moving involuntarily to her chest to touch Spencer's ring through her shirt. "I think I do. It wouldn't hurt so much otherwise." A short, bitter laugh came out of her. "Not that it matters anymore."

"Bullshit," Luna said. "Love always matters."

THE FIRST TIME KIMBERLEIGH TRIED CALLING SPENCER, IT went straight to voicemail. Which meant either his phone was off, he'd declined her call, or he'd blocked her number. Since she'd never known him to turn his phone off, her money was on the second one—although option number three was a definite possibility.

She didn't trust herself to leave a coherent voicemail, so she hung up and texted him instead. It took her a good fifteen minutes and about ten false starts to compose the two-sentence text.

I owe you an apology. Would you be willing to call me so we can talk?

He didn't call back for four and a half hours. Almost midnight Kimberleigh's time, which meant it was nine on the West Coast—the time he often got home from work. She'd been in bed, but wide-awake as usual with her phone lying next to her in case he called.

When it rang, she bolted upright, her heart beating a million miles an hour. She stared at Spencer's face on the screen, taking a deep breath before answering.

"Spencer." Despite the deep breath, her voice cracked a little.

There was a pause long enough that she wondered if he was going to speak at all before he finally said, "Kimber-leigh." That smooth, deep voice with a hint of Georgia drawl shot through her with a surge of relief. But the way he said her name sounded off. Instead of carrying layers of hidden meaning, it hung there flat between them. Empty of all emotion. "You said you wanted to talk."

She hated that sound in his voice, but she'd called for a reason, and it didn't have anything to do with making herself feel better. "I know it wasn't you who leaked the story. I know you were telling the truth."

"Great." That was all he said. Just that one word, so cold and sarcastic it landed in her stomach like a ball of lead. It didn't sound at all like the Spencer she knew.

He was protecting himself from her. Good for him. But it hurt even more than she'd anticipated.

She cleared her throat before reciting the speech she'd been rehearsing in her head for hours. "I'm so sorry. I should have believed you. It wasn't fair, how I treated you. You didn't deserve it, and I can't even express how deeply I regret it, how much I wish I could take it back. I know I can't, but I just wanted you to know how sorry I am."

As grovels went, it wasn't very impressive. She'd given far better speeches on-screen.

There was another pause, shorter this time, like he was waiting to make sure she was done. "All right," he said. "Thank you for telling me."

Thank you for telling me. Like she'd just informed him his hired car was waiting outside. So perfunctory. So detached.

"Spencer—"

"Is that all?" he asked, the brusqueness in his voice as close as he'd come to showing emotion.

"I—" She hadn't been prepared for him to react like this. Of all the scenarios she'd imagined, for some reason she'd never envisioned him being curt. Angry? Aggrieved? Resentful? Sure. But not this flat, disinterested blankness. She cast around for something else to say, afraid this might be the last time they ever spoke. "Are you okay?" she finally settled on weakly.

"I'm...fine," he answered, not quite so terse this time,

the little hesitation in the middle making her think he'd almost said something else. Like he'd almost been tempted to let her in a little. But then he hadn't. He'd gone with *fine* instead. Which meant he obviously wasn't fine at all.

"Spencer," she breathed, her voice shaking with regret. "I messed up. I didn't trust that anything could be that good, so I threw us away. And I'm sorry for fucking it all up. I'm just so incredibly sorry." She ended on a wet, choking sob that finally broke through his protective shield.

"I know." His voice was soft and sympathetic, like he really did understand exactly how wretched she felt. "I know you are."

Maybe there was hope for them after all?

A fat tear slid down her cheek and she reached up to wipe it away. "I just—is there any way—I mean, do you think you might ever be able to—"

"Forgive you?" he offered quietly.

"Give me another chance," she countered. Because that was what she really wanted. She wanted him back. She wanted to fix this. To show him that she could be better. Worthy of him.

His voice was gentle, but his answer cut the legs out from under her. "I don't think that's a good idea."

"Oh." She blinked, squeezing her lips together to stifle another sob.

"Kimberleigh." This time when he said her name, she could hear in it everything he was feeling. All the hurt, the regret, the sorrow. And beneath all that she could hear the love that was still there. The love that hadn't completely gone away yet. "I don't want you to beat yourself up about this. I forgive you, okay? I know why you reacted the way you did. I understand, really I do. I just don't think you're ever going to be able to fully trust me—because of who I am and who you are. And that's not your fault, but I can't be in a relationship like that. I don't think it's good for me."

But I love you.

She almost said it. Her mouth opened to speak the words, but all she said was, "Okay."

"Are you?"

She ignored his question in order to throw one last Hail Mary pass. "What if I promised to be better?"

"Don't," he breathed, like the idea caused him pain. "Don't do that. You don't need to be better. You're perfect the way you are."

You're not a burden. You're a gift. Her heart constricted, remembering when he'd said those words to her. But he didn't think she was a gift anymore, did he?

"We're just not perfect together," he finished sadly. "It's not anyone's fault. It's just what it is."

But I love you. I love you I love you I love you. The words screamed inside her head, but she couldn't make herself say them to him. It felt too desperate. Too manipulative.

She swallowed them down and said, "If that's how you feel."

"That's how I feel."

He sounded so calm. So certain. This was what he wanted. She'd given him a choice, and this was the one he'd made. All that was left for her to do was respect it.

"Right," she said, forcing steadiness into her voice. "Okay. Then I guess this is goodbye."

"I'm sorry."

"No reason for you to be sorry. Take care, Spencer. I

mean that. I hope you get everything you want out of life. You deserve it."

"Kimberleigh—"

"Goodbye." She hung up before he could say anything else, so she didn't break down crying over the phone.

It was for the best.

That was what she told herself over and over again in the days that followed. He'd made the right choice by choosing to protect himself.

Good for him.

That still left the problem of his ring. She felt bad about holding on to it, but since it was only one small thing in a long list of big things she felt bad about where Spencer was concerned, she added that guilt to the rest of it.

After she got back to LA, then she'd figure it out. Have Luna deliver the ring to his office, maybe. Make sure he got it back safe and sound.

In the meantime, Kimberleigh continued to carry it with her every day. The last little piece of Spencer she had left.

She tried to let him go, otherwise. Tried to move on with her life. Even agreed to go out for drinks with some of her castmates to distract herself.

When she was alone at night, her feelings for Spencer threatened to smother her. They made her bones ache with longing and her chest constrict with shame.

Her insomnia was worse than ever. She used the time alone with her thoughts to compose long, heartfelt apologies to Spencer in her head and imagine how her last conversation with him might have gone differently. Sometimes in these imaginings he'd forgive her and welcome her back into his life. But sometimes he'd respond with anger, saying all the awful, hurtful things she knew she deserved.

She wondered if he was okay. Hoped he was moving on with his life. Hoped her betrayal hadn't broken any of his sweetness.

When Kimberleigh's publicist proposed a new faux-mance to help change the narrative about her in the press, she agreed—though not without a moment of hesitation, wondering what Spencer would think.

Probably nothing. Why would he care what she did anymore?

If he was smart, he wouldn't think about her at all.

sixteen

"WELL?" Vanessa asked, following Spencer into his office. "How'd it go?"

He shrugged noncommittally as he sat down at his desk. "Pretty well, I think."

Vanessa stood on the other side of his desk and rested her fingers on the edge. Her fingernails were long and painted dark blue with a different tiny constellation drawn on each one. "Pretty well?" she repeated impatiently. "That's all I get? What's your gut say? Do you think they're going to offer it to you?"

They had offered it to him, in fact. The network's open late-night slot was his, if he wanted it. He ought to be happy about that—ecstatic, even. Six months ago he would have said it was what he wanted most in the world. But he couldn't seem to muster much enthusiasm now—not even enough to accept the job.

Spencer had told them he needed to think about it. His agent was going to kill him, but he just wasn't sure he wanted it anymore.

Truthfully, he hadn't wanted much of anything lately. Not since his breakup with Kimberleigh. Work used to be his driving force, his purpose, the thing that got him out of bed in the morning. But his heart wasn't in it these days. It was too busy trying to stitch itself back together.

"I really don't know," he lied to Vanessa. "We'll have to see." He didn't want to get her hopes up in case he decided to turn it down.

A late-night slot was supposed to be the brass ring for a guy like Spencer. His own studio, his own house band, his name in the title of the show. Wasn't that what everyone wanted? Perform well in the 1:30 a.m. slot, and you were well-positioned to inherit the coveted 12:30 or even 11:30 slots when one of them eventually opened up.

The problem was that the network wanted to keep him in his anchor spot on *Hot Hollywood Nights* and use it to cross-promote with the new late-night show, which would mean two tapings per day, five days a week. To make it work, Spencer would have to give up the morning show segment and his radio show, plus the two cable reality shows he hosted.

The cable gigs he couldn't care less about, but the others were a different matter. The in-depth sit-down interviews he did for the morning show segment and his satellite radio program were the work he was proudest of in his career to date. Sure, the late-night show would be mostly interviews, but it was only a half-hour slot for two guests plus an opening and closing monologue. How in-depth would he be able to get in that kind of format? He'd have five minutes max with each guest to pimp their latest project and not much else.

Was that really what he wanted to spend the next few years doing? Was it worth the long hours that ate up his whole life to the exclusion of almost everything else?

Before Kimberleigh came along, Spencer had lived for work. But she'd shown him there were things he cared about more than his career. Companionship. Comfort. Love. He still wanted those things, even if he couldn't have them with her.

That was why he'd ended things between them for good. It had been the hardest decision he'd ever had to make, and he still second-guessed it every day. Loving her had made him realize how much he needed love in his life. How empty his world had been before she came into it. How much he'd been missing out on by living only for work. Now that he'd let love into his life, he couldn't go back to the way things were before.

But that meant accepting Kimberleigh didn't love him the way he loved her and never would. He'd fooled himself into believing she'd get there, but he couldn't keep holding out for a miracle anymore. She'd never be able to trust him. She had good reasons, and he didn't blame her for it. It was just bad luck, really. He was the wrong person for her. She needed someone who made her feel safe. Someone she trusted enough to let inside the protective walls she'd constructed around herself. He wanted her to have that, but he needed to accept she'd never have it with him.

That was why he'd had to let her go. If he clung to her like he'd wanted to, neither of them would ever find the love they deserved.

God, it had been hard though. Hearing her voice break like that over the phone. The sound of her choking back a sob still haunted him. She'd practically begged him to take her back. And he'd wanted to. Badly. He missed her so much it felt like a piece of himself was missing. Like someone had dug a hole through his chest and scooped out a huge chunk of his heart. He'd never felt as lonely in his whole life as he had this last month. Which was saying something, considering how lonely his life had been up until now.

As if that wasn't bad enough, he'd had to report on Kimberleigh's new romance. Even though he knew it was just a PR stunt, he'd barely been able to get through the script.

"Spencer?" Vanessa tapped one of her constellation nails on the edge of his desk. "Are you okay?"

He looked up at her and forced a smile. "Yeah, I'm fine. Why?"

When she frowned at him, he had the sense she was seeing through all his bullshit. "You haven't seemed like yourself for a while. You've been…I don't know. Subdued, I guess. I thought you'd be more excited about this opportunity."

A pang of guilt nailed him in the solar plexus. It'd be good for Vanessa if he took the late-night gig. More prestige and money for him meant more prestige and money for her.

"I think the long hours have started to get to me," he admitted, sitting back and scrubbing a tired hand over his face. "I've been feeling sort of burned out lately. But I'll be fine," he assured her. "It'll pass. I just need to create a little more work-life balance for myself."

She nodded, seeming to accept this. "You do work too

much. It's not healthy. When's the last time you even took a vacation?"

He laughed hollowly. "I can't remember." It wasn't like he had anyone to take a vacation with, and he'd never seen the point of going on a vacation alone.

"You should really think about taking some time off."

"I will," he promised. "It's a good suggestion."

What would he even do? It wasn't like he had any hobbies to occupy his time. He basically had nothing going for him outside of work.

Vanessa studied him for a long moment, her dark chocolate eyes sharp under her long lashes. "You know, if this late-night hosting thing is going to be too much added stress, maybe you shouldn't do it. Life's too short to work yourself to death."

Spencer bit down on his lip so it wouldn't quiver. God, he'd been so emotional lately. "I'll take that under advisement."

One way or another, he was getting Vanessa a raise. If he turned down the late-night job, he'd find a way to make it up to her.

"Anyway," she said, tapping her nails on the desk again. "Tamara Williams's assistant called while you were out. And you'll never guess why."

He ignored the painful twinge in his chest at the mention of Kimberleigh's publicist. Tamara had a large roster of high-profile clients, and Kimberleigh was only one of them. He had a long-standing and mutually beneficial working relationship with Tamara. She threw him scoops and exclusives when she could, and in exchange he lobbed softballs when one of her celebrity clients got into hot water and wanted to use him as a stop on their apology tour.

"Why?" he asked, trying to look interested.

"To offer you an exclusive interview with Kimberleigh Cress."

All the breath left his body. It was a good thing he was sitting down, because he wasn't sure his legs would have been able to support him.

"I know," Vanessa said. "I was as shocked as you. I guess you're off the blacklist for real, huh? Unless they're punking you. Tamara doesn't strike me as the punking type though."

Spencer cleared his throat to make sure his voice still worked. "Did she mention what the interview is about?"

"Nope. Just that you should let them know if you're interested."

"Can you get Tamara on the phone for me?"

Tamara turned out to be in a meeting, so Spencer had to wait for a call back. Forty-five agonizing minutes later, he finally heard from her.

"I thought that might get your attention," Tamara said, sounding pleased with herself.

"What's this about?" he asked. "Why is Kimberleigh offering me an exclusive interview?"

"Does it matter?"

"It matters to me, yeah." His teeth ground together, and he forced himself to unclench his jaw before he ruined his veneers.

"Kimberleigh hasn't made a public appearance since that story about her childhood came out. But now she's ready to go on the record and talk about it."

"Does she know you're offering the interview to me?"

"This was her idea. I'm just giving my client what she wants. If you're not interested—"

"I didn't say that. What kind of format are we talking about? Is this for my morning show segment or—"

"Undetermined. She wants to meet with you first to talk about the format and ground rules."

Okaaaay.

What the fuck was she up to?

She could have simply called him and asked to talk if that was what she wanted.

"It's a little unusual, I know," Tamara added in response to Spencer's silence. "But I'm sure you can understand this is a difficult subject for her to talk about, and she wants to do it on her terms. Can I tell her you're in?"

"Yes," he said. "Tell her I'll meet with her."

seventeen

SPENCER HAD NEVER BEEN this nervous about a meeting with an interview subject in his life. He'd barely slept for the last week, thinking about seeing Kimberleigh again and wondering how she'd act toward him. Would she be chilly? Wounded? Indifferent?

He'd started to call her a hundred times to ask her what the hell this was all about. But every single time he'd chickened out, afraid if they talked, the conversation would go badly. What if they argued and wound up hurting each other again?

At least this way Tamara would be present for their meeting, which would forestall any discussion of personal matters. They'd talk about the interview, agree on a format, and that would be that.

This will be fine.

Maybe it was all exactly what it seemed. Just business. Kimberleigh had felt the need to do an interview and decided Spencer was the person she trusted most to do it. Which—he couldn't lie—made him feel some kind of way.

Did it mean he'd been wrong? That she was capable of trusting him after all? If that was true, then—

No.

He couldn't think about that. Not right now. Right now he had to focus on getting through this meeting with his professionalism and dignity intact.

Of course, it didn't help that the location Tamara had picked for the meeting was a suite at the same Santa Monica hotel where the Tinsel & Tatas Gala had been held last year. Spencer was also feeling some kind of way about that as he rode up the very same elevator he'd ridden with Kimberleigh after her panic attack.

He got off on the same floor he'd escorted Kimberleigh to that night. What an odd thing to remember—the floor her room had been on. But he remembered everything about that night. Her dress, her perfume, the very first time she'd betrayed a hint of a smile. That one strand of hair that had worked its way loose after she'd leaned against him and let him hold her in his arms.

Fuck.

Thinking about shit like that would only make this harder.

Professional detachment. That was what he needed. It was the only way he was going to get through the next hour.

Tamara opened the door at Spencer's knock and invited him inside. It was a roomy suite with a sitting area and an ocean view. The balcony door was open, admitting a warm, sea-scented breeze. There was no sign of Kimberleigh.

Maybe she won't be here after all.

He shouldn't be so disappointed about that. What had he actually expected? That this whole thing was an elaborate setup to get him back? That Kimberleigh would beg him to give her another chance, and this time he'd agree?

Yes.

That was exactly what he'd been hoping. Like a goddamn fool.

"Settle in." Tamara waved him toward the sitting area as she moved to the minibar. "Can I get you a drink?"

"I wouldn't mind a water," Spencer said, situating himself in an uncomfortable blue armchair. As soon as Tamara turned her back, he ran a finger under the collar of his shirt. He was sweating, and not because of the weather in Santa Monica today.

As he leaned forward to accept a bottle of Fiji water from Tamara, he heard a door open behind him. He didn't have to look to know it was Kimberleigh. He could feel her presence the second she entered the room—a change in the air as distinctive as the sea breeze coming in from the balcony.

Distant and professional, he reminded himself as he got to his feet.

He turned around, and his senses completely abandoned him the second his gaze tangled with Kimberleigh's. His feet tried to walk toward her automatically—unthinkingly— before he remembered himself and made them stop.

The sight of her was so beautiful—and so painful—it almost brought tears to his eyes. He recognized the loose, flowery dress she wore. He knew exactly how that gauzy fabric felt under his fingers, and remembered untying that sash around her waist as he'd laid her back on her bed a few months ago.

"Thank you for coming," Kimberleigh said as if Spencer

was merely an acquaintance and not someone who'd willingly die on a battlefield for her.

One of them was acing the professional detachment thing, and it sure as hell wasn't him.

There was a moment of silence, during which Spencer was distantly aware it was his turn to speak. Everyone was waiting for him to reply to Kimberleigh's greeting, but he couldn't make himself do it. He didn't know what he was supposed to say to her, how to respond to such a banal statement when his half-healed heart was tearing itself in two all over again.

Kimberleigh's gaze shifted over his shoulder. "Tamara, can you give us fifteen minutes, please? I need to speak to Spencer alone before we start."

"I really don't think that's a good idea." Tamara sounded surprised and rightfully alarmed. Clearly Kimberleigh hadn't clued her in to whatever was going on.

"It's okay." Kimberleigh's eyes drifted back to Spencer. "You don't have anything to worry about. Nothing we say will leave this room."

"Kimberleigh—"

"I'm afraid I have to insist." Kimberleigh was looking at Tamara again, the steel in her voice matching her eyes. "Fifteen minutes. That's all we'll need."

That's all we'll need.

The words dropped through Spencer like a stone. What did Kimberleigh want to say to him that would only take fifteen minutes?

Certainly not what he'd hoped to hear. Once again he felt like a fool for letting himself get his hopes up. Maybe Kimberleigh just wanted some closure, or even just to establish boundaries for their future professional inter-actions.

Only grudgingly did Tamara leave them alone, and only after Kimberleigh walked her to the door. When the suite door slammed closed behind her, Spencer realized he still hadn't moved. Slowly, he turned to face Kimberleigh again.

"Why am I here?" he asked, finally finding his voice. "What is this?"

Kimberleigh walked toward him without speaking. It took all his self control not to reach for her as she drew nearer. Her eyes locked onto his, and he felt the air leave his lungs.

"I need to give this back to you." She reached for his hand, uncurled his fingers, and pressed something warm and metal into his palm.

He looked down at his grandfather's ring with a crushing sense of disappointment. So this was about closure after all. She'd brought him here to tidy up the loose ends and pack the last artifacts of their relationship into mothballs.

It was too bad, really. Because the second she touched him, he knew with absolute certainty that she was all he was ever going to want. No one would ever compare or matter as much. She'd inked herself over the surface of his heart like a tattoo, and there was no room left for anyone else.

The epiphany startled a small, slightly hysterical-sounding laugh out of him. Kimberleigh stiffened, her eyes blinking away from him as she started to withdraw her hand.

He didn't let her. His fingers closed around hers of their own accord, even before he'd consciously decided to do it.

He couldn't make himself let go of her. He'd already done it once, and it had nearly destroyed him. There was no way he'd survive it a second time.

"Kimberleigh…" His throat clogged, swallowing the last half of her name. He hadn't thought of anything to say beyond that anyway, so he just kept clinging to her hand, holding it and his grandfather's ring together.

His thumb rubbed over her knuckles, seeking comfort but also offering it. She looked down at where their hands were touching. Her eyes fluttered closed, then open again. Taking hold of herself, she slipped her hand out of his and backed a more respectable distance away.

Spencer jammed the ring into his pocket, feeling bereft. "Is that all this is about? You could have messengered it to me."

Kimberleigh's lips pressed together, and she gave a small shake of her head. "No, you're here because of the interview. I just thought we should talk before we get down to business. Clear the air, I guess."

"All right." He squeezed his fist around the ring in his pocket until it hurt. "Let's clear the air then, starting with this interview—I don't understand why you want to do it."

"Tamara thinks I need to. And I think she's right. My past is public now and ignoring it won't make it go away." Kimberleigh's gaze dropped to the floor as her fingers twisted the sash of her dress. She inhaled a breath and said, "I think it's time I tried being a little less guarded."

Spencer tried not to read too much into that last sentence, because reading too much into this interaction had already left him feeling bruised. "If that's what you want, fine. But I still don't understand why you'd want me for it."

She looked up at him. "Why wouldn't I want you? You're the only person I can trust."

He swallowed thickly, trying to hold it together but not managing it very well at all, and he was grateful when she did him the favor of lowering her eyes to the floor again.

"But also I wanted to do something for you," she said, sounding uncharacteristically hesitant. "Something…nice, I guess, as a way of—I don't know—making amends? It sounds dumb now that I'm saying it out loud. Maybe it was a mistake. But you've done so much for me, I wanted to help you somehow, even though I know you don't need my help. And this exclusive was all I could think of to give you that you might still want."

Her knuckles were white as she continued to wring her sash in her hands, her eyes downcast so he couldn't see her expression. But in the silence he could hear her swallow and inhale a sharp, shaky breath.

She was crying, he realized with a stab of panic.

"I'm sorry." She reached up to swipe a hand under her eyes. "This is even harder than I thought it would be."

"What is?" His voice was faint and unsteady, and it took all the self-control he had not to go to her and fold her into his arms. He still wasn't sure if she'd want that. Hope kept trying to flare in his chest, but he was so wary of being burned again that he tried to tamp it down.

"There's so much I want to say to you, I don't know where to start." Kimberleigh shook her head as if she was trying to clear her thoughts. When she looked up at him again, her shining emerald eyes were the brightest things in the room. "Before you, it was like I was living alone on an island, because that was what I needed to do to survive. I thought I was safer alone, where no one could reach me. But then you swooped in to rescue me when I had that panic attack. And you kept right on trying to rescue me over and over, every minute we were together. You tried your damnedest to drag me off that island."

Spencer's heart was beating too fast. This was all so much and his head was spinning with everything she'd said. He was overwhelmed, confused, and terrified of what it was leading to. Afraid she was only here for closure. That all of this was just the prologue to a final *thanks for the memories* and *have a nice life*.

"I should have held on to you with both hands," she continued, clutching that sash like it was a security blanket. "But I didn't trust what I felt, and that's my fault. I was too afraid to believe what you showed me, so I gave up on you the second it got hard. You deserved better than that. You're the best person I've ever known, Spencer. I wish I'd realized sooner how much I love you."

The last three words caught him off guard. He had to go back and replay them in his head to be sure he hadn't imagined it. But no. She'd said the thing he'd never expected to hear. He'd been torturing himself the last month, aching for her and denying himself hope. Grieving the loss of her. But he'd been wrong about everything. So wrong. Because she loved him. She *loved* him.

He swallowed around the lump rising in his throat. "Kimberleigh—"

A brisk, determined shake of her head silenced him. "I don't expect anything from you. You've already done so much for me. I know I ruined everything, and it's something I'll regret forever. But you changed my life, and you have no idea how grateful I'll always be for that. You showed me what I was missing and taught me that love was worth taking risks. That's why I chose this location for this meeting. Because this hotel is where I first started living again. Because of *you*. And I want you to know I'll always love you, so if you ever need anything—"

She didn't get to finish, because by then Spencer had crossed the room and taken her face in his hands. "Stop," he whispered, stroking his thumb across her cheek. "Just stop. You're all I'll ever need."

The beginning of a hesitant smile curved her lips, and he set his mouth against hers. It was like a first kiss—tender, exploring, full of relief and wonder. Kimberleigh's hands smoothed up his sides, and he leaned in closer, his whole body yearning for more contact. Holding her felt so natural, like it was what he'd been made to do.

When they finally broke apart, she laid her hand on his chest right over his thudding heart. "I thought I'd lost you for good."

"I'm so sorry," he said. When she shook her head, he laid his hand over hers, holding it against his chest the way he'd done that night eight months ago. "I gave up on you too. When you called to apologize, I should have given you another chance. For all my big talk about trust, I was just as afraid as you were.

Kimberleigh smiled and leaned forward to kiss him again. "Let's just say we've both got some work to do."

"We'll work on it together. From now on, you and me are a team." He wrapped his arms around her, pulling her close, enjoying the feel of her body against his and the perfect way they fit together.

She nuzzled into his neck and took a deep breath like she was inhaling him. "I like the sound of that."

"But listen, this interview—"

"I still want to do it." She pulled back to look at him. "And I want to do it with you, if you're willing."

"Are you sure?"

She nodded and tipped her head toward him, snuggling close again. "I meant what I said. It's time I let some of my walls down. And there's no one I trust to help me through that conversation as much as you."

"I love you," he said for the first time with her in his arms, and he felt something loosen inside him that had been knotted for as long as he could remember. Standing there in that hotel suite with a warm breeze blowing through the room, the sound of the sea behind him, and Kimberleigh in his arms, was the happiest Spencer had ever felt.

"I love you too," she mumbled against his chest, and he realized he was wrong.

This was the happiest he'd ever been.

He pulled back just far enough to touch his thumb under her chin and tip her head up. As his lips touched hers, he thought about how lucky he was, and how if he played his cards right he'd be able to keep kissing Kimberleigh Cress like this for the rest of his life.

When the door to the suite opened a few minutes later, things between them had gotten considerably more heated, and they were leading off second base and threatening to steal third.

"What? The *fuck*?" Tamara demanded as they guiltily jumped apart.

"Um…" Spencer ducked his head, grimacing at the

awkwardness. When he looked down he saw his shirt was half untucked.

Kimberleigh's hand slipped confidently into his. "Tamara, in the interest of full disclosure, you should know that Spencer and I are together and have been seeing each other for over six months."

Tamara crossed her arms, regarding them with narrowed eyes for what felt to Spencer like a hundred years. "Are you planning to go public?" she asked finally.

Spencer and Kimberleigh exchanged a wordless look.

"I don't think so," Kimberleigh said, turning back to Tamara. "Maybe one day, but it's better to keep it under wraps for now."

"I'm sure the actor Kimberleigh's supposed to be dating right now will be glad to hear that," Tamara said with a roll of her eyes.

When Kimberleigh snorted, Spencer couldn't suppress his grin any longer. She was just so fucking perfect. And she loved him. He was never going to stop grinning over that.

Tamara rolled her eyes again as she sank down in one of the blue armchairs. "Are we having this meeting or what?"

FIVE YEARS LATER

"KIMBERLEIGH?" Spencer called through the bedroom door. "You haven't climbed out the window, have you?"

Kimberleigh met Luna's eyes in the mirror and they shared a smile. "Yes," she called back, wincing as Luna shoved another bobby pin into her hair. "I'm currently shimmying my way over the security gate to meet up with the getaway car waiting around the corner to whisk me away to freedom."

She'd kicked Spencer out of their bedroom two hours ago so she could get ready without him hovering around. He'd had to get dressed down the hall in the guest room, which had likely only taken him twenty minutes, because men had it criminally easy.

"Very funny." Spencer sounded tense, which she found adorable. "It's time. Past time, as a matter of fact."

"Just a minute," Luna snapped as she poked at Kimberleigh's hair, checking to make sure the intricate network of bobby pins would hold. "You can't rush perfection."

"He's nervous," Kimberleigh mouthed at Luna, who was the only friend she and Spencer had let in on the secret reason for today's gathering.

"Men," Luna replied, shaking her head. "So emotional."

Kimberleigh stood up, balancing with a hand on the wall as she slipped into her shoes. "I guess you'd better let him in before he melts down in the hallway."

"Our guests are starting to wonder where you are," Spencer was saying. "They're not going to hang around forever waiting, you know. And I'm sure you look—"

Luna threw open the bedroom door, and Spencer's gaze homed in on Kimberleigh like a heat-seeking missile.

"—beautiful," he breathed as his frown melted away.

"Really?" she asked, doing a twirl in her gauzy white sundress. "You're not just saying that because you want me to hurry?"

"Kimberleigh." As he came toward her, his mouth curved in a slow, devastating smile that made her heart do that swoopy thing it still did even after five straight years of Spencer's devastating smiles. "You're the most beautiful thing I've ever seen."

"You don't look so bad yourself." She smoothed her hands over the lapels of his light gray suit, feeling like the luckiest woman in the world. "I can't believe a guy as hunky as you is still single. Someone should snap you up and put a ring on it."

"Maybe one of these days someone will." His tone was playful, but his expression had gone taut again.

"I'll leave you two alone for a minute," Luna said, slipping out of the room. "See you downstairs for the big event."

Kimberleigh hooked a thumb over her shoulder as she gazed up at Spencer. "The window's right there if you want to make a break for it. There's still time to get away if you're having second thoughts."

"No." He took her hand and straightened the diamond engagement ring he'd given her two years ago. She'd only ever worn it when they were at home, but after today she'd finally be able to show it off in public. "No second thoughts. I'm ready for this. So ready."

"Okay," she said, squeezing his hand. "But...?"

Spencer blew out an unsteady breath. "It's just nerves— but the good kind, you know? Anticipatory nerves. This is a huge step we're about to take."

"It is," Kimberleigh agreed solemnly.

"Aren't you even a little nervous?"

She took his hand and pressed his palm against her chest, holding it there so he could feel the way her heart was pounding. "You feel that?"

He nodded, smiling.

"It's all for you."

His smile grew wider as he bent down, tilting his head—

"No kissing!" she said, shoving him away. "Not until after."

He huffed in frustration. "I kissed you two hours ago."

"That was before I put on the dress. No kissing in the dress until it's official."

"Fine, then let's go make it official," he said and herded her out of their bedroom.

When they got downstairs, they paused and gazed through the picture windows at the guests assembled in the back garden. All their closest friends were here, mingling around the pool as they sipped champagne. The invitations hadn't listed any occasion for the party, but Kimberleigh suspected more than a few of their friends had sussed out what was up.

This day had been over five years in the making. Five years of secrets, discretion, and pretending in order to keep their private lives private. But now, finally, they were taking their relationship public by making it official. A new beginning. A new life together. All their dreams come true.

Their wedding day.

"Are you ready to do this?" Kimberleigh asked, smiling up at Spencer.

He beamed back at her. "I've never been readier for anything in my whole life."

She slipped her hand in his, and they stepped out into the sunlight together.

HHN Exclusive: Kimberleigh Cress and Spencer Devlin's Secret Wedding Surprise!

Two-time Oscar nominee Kimberleigh Cress married talk show host Spencer Devlin this weekend in a wedding that was a surprise to everyone— including the guests! This adorable Hollywood couple tied the knot Saturday in an intimate ceremony at their home in Los Angeles, HHN has confirmed.

Reportedly, the friends and loved ones who showed up for the couple's special day had no idea they'd been invited to a wedding. "The invitations just said to come for brunch and cocktails," our source told us.

The secret wedding came on the heels of a lengthy engagement, which the couple also kept secret from all but an inner circle of friends. How Cress and Devlin managed to elude the paparazzi and keep their relationship under wraps for so long is a mystery, but it shows just how seriously the couple takes their privacy. Although they've attended many of the same industry events over the years, most recently the Academy Awards in April, they've never been photographed together or romantically linked in the press.

A former *Hot Hollywood Nights* TV anchor, Devlin is currently the host of the Netflix celebrity interview show *Up Close and Personal with Spencer Devlin*, as well as the author of a *New York Times* bestselling memoir, *It's All an Illusion*. Cress, who shot to stardom with the megahit *Otherwhere* film trilogy, can next be seen on the big screen in September, starring opposite Oscar-winner Scott Deacon in *Anacostia Station*, the highly anticipated Cold War drama from filmmaker Joe Lincoln.

A SNEAK PEEK

Lights, camera, attraction...

Combative coworkers go from enemies to lovers when sparks fly behind the camera in this Hollywood comeback story.

"So it's really Scotty Deacon?" Carmen asked.

Grace Speer looked up from her desk in the empty bullpen of the *Sunset Limited* production offices. It was late, and nearly everyone else had called it quits for the day, except Carmen Vargas, who'd just wandered over from the costume department office down the hall.

"It's really Scotty Deacon." Grace's lips curled a little as they formed the words. "He's coming in tonight to meet with Joe." She glanced at the clock on the wall. "In about ten minutes."

After months of searching, a string of disappointing auditions, and two failed negotiations, the producers had finally cast the lead of *Sunset Limited*, the indie neo-noir thriller that was due to start principal photography next month in New Orleans.

Grace could only assume the decision to give the part to Scotty Deacon had been made out of desperation. It was the only reason she could think why they'd agreed to cast a washed-up former teen heartthrob who hadn't worked in years.

"Huh." Carmen held a pad of costume sketches in one hand and a cup of coffee in the other as she leaned against the edge of Grace's desk. "I thought he was dead."

Grace had thought the same thing until she'd seen his name on the short list for *Sunset Limited*.

Scotty Deacon had been one of the rare Disney Channel stars to make the transition from tween heartthrob to big-time box office hunk—until a messy drug habit, a string of DUIs, and enough bad behavior to earn him his own episode of *E! True Hollywood Story* had derailed his career. After getting himself fired from the set of a Michael Bay film four years ago, Deacon had been blacklisted in Hollywood and dropped off the radar completely. Grace could have sworn she'd heard something about an overdose a couple years back, but she must have been mixing up her former child stars.

"Only figuratively," she told Carmen. "He's looking to make a comeback, apparently."

Carmen's eye roll conveyed her skepticism. "And we're the chumps who get to take a chance on the drug addict? Lucky us." As costume supervisor, Carmen had to get up close and personal with all the actors, but especially with the lead, who would be in nearly every scene of the film and would therefore require the most costumes and costume changes.

"Recovering addict," Grace corrected. "Joe says he's been working the program for two years now. Turned over a new leaf or something."

Not that she believed a word of it. She trusted Joe Lincoln—he was one of her preferred directors to work with —but he had an optimist's tendency to think the best of everyone that Grace didn't share. Because she liked Joe so much, she hated to think of him being taken in by a self-destructive burnout whose dumpster fire of a personal life could bring the entire production to a screeching halt.

What surprised Grace was that Joe's producing partner and wife, Nichole, had ever agreed to cast Deacon—an actor with a well-documented history of showing up to set so high he couldn't say his lines without an earpiece when he even both-ered to show up at all. Nichole was the pragmatic business-minded half of the partnership who kept the ship afloat and cleaned up messes before they could turn into full-fledged disas-ters. The fact that she'd agreed to take on Scotty Deacon meant he'd either made one hell of a convincing case for himself, or they were so desperate Nichole hadn't had any other choice.

"I thought he was uninsurable," Carmen said, dragging a chair over from a nearby desk.

That was the main reason Deacon hadn't worked in four years. Once the insurance companies determined you were high-risk, the insane premiums tended to dissuade producers from taking a chance on you.

"Everyone's insurable if you've got enough money to pay for it." Grace cut a glance at the closed door to Joe's office and lowered her voice. "A friend of his put up the bond out of his own pocket."

Carmen's eyes widened as she fiddled with the height adjustment on the chair to accommodate her short frame. "Who?"

"Robbie Scarborough."

"Wow. Okay, then."

Robbie Scarborough had hit it big around the same time as Scotty, and for a while the two of them had run in the same pack of young Hollywood actors charmingly nicknamed the "Coochie Squad"—until they'd had a big falling out a few years ago. But if Robbie was personally bankrolling Scotty's comeback, they must have patched things up.

"Must be nice to have a friend willing to risk a few mil to get you a job, huh?" Carmen said sourly.

"Yeah," Grace agreed, unable to imagine a friendship worth handing over that kind of money. "Must be." She clicked her retractable pen as she glanced at the clock again. "The schedule's already tight, and I know the budget's stretched to the max, so if Deacon starts pulling his usual crap again…"

Carmen shook her head as she sipped her coffee. "Didn't he throw a chair at a director once?"

"Yeah, he did." Grace had done some reading up on Deacon after Joe told her he'd been cast in the lead, and what she'd learned had only intensified her misgivings. The guy hadn't just thrown a chair at Jerry Duncan, the two of them had gotten into an on-set shoving match that had devolved into a full-on brawl before the crew managed to pull them off each other.

Grace's job as script supervisor required her to be the director's near-constant companion, sitting next to him and taking meticulous notes on every take—time codes, lenses, camera movements, props, costumes—to ensure continuity when the footage was cut together in editing. That meant watching the actors closely and noting every detail of their performance: every action they made, when it happened and where, how they were sitting or standing, when and how they handled the props.

When an actor forgot a line or stage direction, Grace was the one who fed it to them, and if they deviated from the script or a previous take, it was her job to point it out. That could involve a lot of interaction with the talent, particularly if they were prone to flubbing lines or missing marks.

A bad apple could make her life a living hell for the duration of the shoot, and Scotty Deacon was one giant honking Red Delicious. If he decided to start throwing furniture or punches on this set, Grace would be right smack in the line of fire.

Carmen shook her head. "Gonna be an interesting shoot."

"I honestly don't know what Joe and Nichole were thinking," Grace said as she clicked her pen. "The guy's never been more than a pretty face, so why take such a big risk on him? There are dozens of actors more talented and more professional than Scotty Deacon. Why not pick one of them instead?"

"They must have their reasons," Carmen said with a shrug. "We'll just have to trust them."

"Yeah," Grace replied without zeal.

Trust wasn't something that came naturally to her. She'd always been too much of a worrier and control freak to embrace the concept of blind faith. As much as she respected Joe and Nichole, she'd sooner trust a clown hiding in a sewer grate than put her fate in the hands of someone like Scotty Deacon.

Scott Deacon stood in the hall outside the production office, frozen in place. He was early for his meeting with Joe Lincoln, which he'd been feeling pretty proud of until the sound of his name had stopped him in his tracks.

Two women inside the office ahead were talking about him, and in less than flattering terms.

He ought to be used to it by now. He had a string of critical and box office successes under his belt, he'd been inducted into the Academy when he was only twenty-six years old, and he had a star on the goddamn Walk of Fame, but all anyone seemed to care about was his mistakes. He had been branded a fuckup by the world at large, and a fuckup he would remain until he'd proven himself otherwise.

That was the whole point of doing this two-bit indie film for union scale. To show the world that Scott Deacon was clean and sober and willing to show up on time every day to do the work. To prove he still had talent and a career left in him.

Scott knew he had a lot to make up for, and he couldn't blame anyone for being reluctant to put their trust in him after all the shit he'd pulled over the years. All most people knew about him was what they'd read: the coke binges and drug psychosis, the run-ins with the law, the multiple stints in rehab. They didn't have any reason to believe that was all in his past, didn't know how hard he'd worked these last two years to finally get himself clean and stay that way. No one was writing articles about healthy, sober Scott Deacon, because the everyday struggle of recovery wasn't as enter-taining as his drug-addled antics had been.

He'd known going into this job that everyone would be scrutinizing him with mistrust, waiting for him to revert to his old habits. He'd been prepared for that, but that wasn't what had stopped him cold in the hall outside Joe Lincoln's office.

The guy's never been more than a pretty face. There are dozens of actors more talented and more professional than Scotty Deacon. Why not pick one of them instead?

Hearing his own worst fears about himself voiced aloud by a stranger was a real punch to the diaphragm. Whoever the woman was, she'd landed a solid hit on Scott's deepest, darkest insecurities—the ones that woke him up at night in a cold sweat.

In his lowest moments, he was convinced he'd never had any real talent in the first place. That the successes he'd achieved in the past had been the net effect of luck, connec-tions, and unearned confidence, and now that all three of those magic elements had abandoned him, he'd be revealed for what he really was: a no-talent waste of space.

Fame had been part of Scott's life for almost as long as he could remember. It had been a protective sheath woven into the fabric of his reality that had shielded him from certain kinds of scrutiny and a lot of the harsher realities of the world. When you were famous, it stopped mattering who you were underneath the fame, because the fame was all anyone cared about or reacted to.

But when that fame slipped away, it left you stripped bare and defenseless in the stark glare of an unforgiving world. Learning to cope with the back end of fame these last few years had been almost as difficult as learning to cope without drugs.

Navigating his recovery and his new reality as a celebrity washout was like kayaking over unfamiliar rapids. He didn't have any control over where the river went or how rough the ride was, so he had to exert his control in whatever small ways he could, by learning safety maneuvers and equipping himself with gear to cushion the blow. He'd had to learn coping mechanisms to manage himself and fill the empty spaces the fame and the drugs used to occupy in his life.

Scott had felt like he'd been doing a pretty decent job steering through the rapids lately, but hearing that woman's words just now, when he was about to meet with the man who'd be directing him in his first film in four years, was like having his kayak overturned by a rock hidden beneath the water's surface.

His hand moved reflexively to the pocket where he used to keep his pills. There was nothing there but gum now. He popped a piece with a shaking hand, trying to pacify the lingering itch for pharmaceutical intervention. Spearmint was a miserable substitute for the soothing, glorious numbness of an opioid high. Without that tranquilizing buffer to protect him from the real world, his brain felt like it was being dragged over a cheese grater.

He closed his eyes and put a hand against the wall as

reality came crashing down around him, crumbling his thin veneer of confidence to dust.

Before anyone inside the office could see him, Scott turned and retreated back the way he'd come, back to the safety of his car where he could pull himself together in private.

———

Grace was still chatting with Carmen in the outer office when Scotty Deacon finally showed up for his meeting with Joe—fifteen minutes late, of course.

After working ten years in the entertainment industry, Grace liked to think she was immune to celebrity. She'd dealt with enough of them, both major and minor, that fame and beauty no longer made much of an impact on her.

But even she had to admit that in person, Scotty Deacon was something extraordinary. It wasn't just his good looks, which were the kind of off-the-Richter-scale gorgeous she'd encountered plenty of times before. It was his *presence*. She couldn't put it into words, but there was something about him, some sort of hypnotic intensity that worked like a supermagnet to pull all the focus in the room.

When Deacon's six-foot frame filled the doorway, he commanded attention without saying a word. Grace found herself sitting up a little straighter as his dark eyes skated over her and Carmen—then quickly dismissed them as insignificant.

"Joe Lincoln?" he demanded in a brusque, *I don't have*

time for niceties tone that dared anyone to waste his time with intrusive chitchat.

Grace lifted her eyebrows along with her pen, and pointed toward the space's only office, which had a piece of white printer paper taped beside the doorframe with the words *JOE LINCOLN* written in large black capital letters.

"Get me a water," Deacon threw over his shoulder as he started for Joe's office. "Sparkling if you have it."

Charming. Grace could already tell working with him was going to be as much fun as a pap smear with a cold speculum.

"Which one of us were you talking to?" Carmen replied coolly as she leaned back in her chair. If her eyes could shoot knives, the back of Scotty Deacon's head would look like a cutlery starter set right about now.

He stopped and turned, fixing them both with a look that reeked of disdain. "I don't care. Whichever one of you is Joe's assistant."

Grace crossed her arms and met his gaze evenly. "That would be neither of us."

One of the first things she'd learned as a script supervisor was not to let herself be intimidated by anyone's entitled, imperious bullshit. Her job and the success of the entire film depended on her not being afraid to speak up when she had something to say, so she couldn't afford to be meek or passive.

What Grace's job *didn't* entail was taking water orders from washed-up cokeheads. If she gave ground now, it would set the tone for the rest of their working relationship, and he would go right on snapping orders at her and expecting to be obeyed.

Before Deacon could reply, the office door opened and Joe Lincoln peeked out. "Scott! I thought I heard your voice out here!" Despite being recently lauded by TheWrap as "the next great Black director," Joe had a down-to-earth attitude and a friendly demeanor that tended to put everyone at their ease. But even his natural warmth couldn't quite take the chill out of the room.

Grace watched as Deacon turned to greet Joe and his scornful expression shifted into an ingratiating smile, smooth as the slide on a dimmer switch. She and Carmen exchanged a look as the two men shook hands.

"You guys all introduce yourselves already?" Joe asked, turning to Grace and Carmen.

"Not yet," Grace said, affixing a saccharine smile to her face as she got to her feet. She could pretend to be nice when the boss was around too.

Joe addressed Deacon as he gestured to Carmen. "This is Carmen Vargas, our costume supervisor."

"Nice to meet you," Carmen said flatly as she stood and shook hands with Deacon.

"And Grace Speer, our script supervisor."

"Hi." Deacon's voice was warm as popcorn butter, though his eyes grew distinctly cold as they focused on Grace.

She kept her expression neutral as she accepted the hand he offered. "So you're the famous Scotty Deacon."

"I prefer Scott."

"Of course you do," Grace said. "My mistake, *Scott.*"

"I'm glad you all could meet." Joe's dimples peeked through his salt-and-pepper beard as he surveyed the three of them. "Since you're going to be spending a lot of time together when production starts."

Scott's eyes bored into Grace with unsettling intensity. The dark, brooding mystique he'd adopted as his post-puberty persona was on maximum display, his hazel-green gaze narrowed and his angular jaw set in a hard line. Most actors looked smaller in real life than on-screen, but Scott had bulked up considerably in his time away from the spotlight, and he struck an imposing figure in person.

Grace's smile grew even wider and more artificial as she stared him down, grateful for every one of the five feet ten inches that put her almost at his level. "Wonderful."

"Can't wait," Carmen said beside her.

Scott turned to Joe, affecting his genial expression again. "Shall we get started?"

"Absolutely! Can I get you a water or anything?"

"No thanks," Scott said as he followed Joe into the office. "I'm good."

"He seems nice," Carmen said dryly after the office door had closed behind them.

"Yeah, he's a real treat," Grace replied, turning to gather her purse. "I'm going home." She'd seen more than enough of Scotty Deacon for one night, and would rather ingest a gallon of live bees than hang around until he came out of Joe's office.

After bidding goodnight to Carmen, Grace collected her things and headed down to the parking lot. The production had rented a suite of second-floor offices in a dire-looking office park in Culver City, sandwiched between a Public Storage and a tile wholesaler. As she stepped outside, she saw an electric blue Tesla that probably cost more than the balance on her student loans parked diagonally across two spaces.

It had to be Deacon's car. Because of course he'd drive something that flashy and park it like a total asshole.

That was who she'd be working with on a near-daily basis for nine weeks in New Orleans starting next month. The guy who couldn't be bothered with common politeness unless the director was standing there, who'd assumed she was an assistant and tried to order her around like a servant, and who'd gifted her with a malevolent glare simply for refusing to be intimidated by him.

Scotty Deacon could get fucked.

Read the rest of Grace and Scott's story in FALLEN STAR...

about the author

SUSANNAH NIX is a RITA® Award-winning and *USA Today* bestselling author of rom-coms and contemporary romances who lives in Texas with her husband. On the rare occasions she's not writing, she can be found reading, knitting, lifting weights, drinking wine, or obsessively watching *Ted Lasso* on repeat to stave off existential angst.

TO LEARN MORE ABOUT SUSANNAH NIX, VISIT:

susannahnix.com

OR FOLLOW HER ON SOCIAL MEDIA:

facebook.com/SusannahNix

twitter.com/Susannah_Nix

instagram.com/susannahnixauthor

bookbub.com/profile/susannah-nix

goodreads.com/susannah_nix

CPSIA information can be obtained
at www.ICGtesting.com
Printed in the USA
LVHW040044290422
717483LV00008B/1237

9 781950 087143